Don't Forget

VALERIE BOWER

ISBN
979-8-88945-349-9 (Paperback)
979-8-88945-350-5 (eBook)

Brilliant Books Literary
137 Forest Park Lane Thomasville
North Carolina 27360 USA

PROLOGUE

Our journey started in back in September of 1985 because that is when your heart started to beat. Of course I didn't know about you until a few weeks later, but I fell in love with you, and a piece of my heart started to grow from that day forward.

I remember the first doctor appointment and being told that I was pregnant. I was so excited I couldn't wait to tell your dad about the appointment and that we had a little baby on the way.

On November 1, I was bleeding and having some cramps. I returned to the doctor for my second appointment. He didn't hear a heartbeat and scheduled me to return the first of December sooner if needed.

I have had a miscarriage, and I know what it feels like. I had a very difficult month from Thanksgiving to Christmas. I was bleeding and had cramps that would not go away.

I began to feel like I would not be able to hold this little child in my arms ever. I was already in love with you. I have been through this loss before, and I didn't want to go through it again. To me, it's almost Christmas, and I didn't want to remember Christmas as losing my baby.

A miracle happened at a church Christmas party, which I had been invited to. I remember the ladies asked if anyone had a prayer request. I raised my hand for prayer. I was willing to share with these women who were strangers to me at the time. So I shared how I had not been feeling well, how the doctor had not been able to hear a heartbeat.

My greatest fear at this time is of losing the baby I had already fallen in love with. The women of the church put their hands on me and prayed for you and me. On Christmas Day, the bleeding stopped.

The Bible says that God is the same yesterday, today, and forever. If he could raise the dead and heal the sick, he could save my baby if it was in his plans.

On my next appointment, the doctor could hear a strong heartbeat. You will never know the joy I felt and the excitement that I was going to have another little baby!

I try to think of the things I want to share about you and your life growing up. There are so many wonderful stories and memories. But I will save them for me.

I want to share the last six months of your life, the struggles we went through, the love shared, and the final day.

This is the piece of my heart I hope will change the lives of people who read this book. I want moms to hold their babies, sisters, and brothers to say "I love you," and families to realize that tomorrow may not come. Every day should have a memory to hang on to.

My cousin had been pregnant the same time I was. She went into labor early and delivered a little boy. He lived for a few days, and then he went to sleep in her arms. I cried for her and prayed she would have the strength to make it through the difficult days to come.

I wrote a poem for my cousin and baby Chad. I never thought then that I too would lose my little baby boy.

A Perfect Child

Just that little kick inside of you that
said "Hey Mom I'm here,
I'm living and breathing and wondering,
Will you always hold me near?
I may not be as perfect as you really did
expect, but God has put me here you see
To give him more respect.
For when you see another child, you're sure to
understand that I was made more precious,
Then any child at hand.
For I will be made perfect in a twinkling of
an eye, and sit in heaven's glory and
Wait for you on high.
Then I will run to greet you, so you can
hold me near. You can tell me
How you love me
By whispering in my ear.

In memory of my son
Jeremy Tim Baumann

June 10, 1986–December 7, 2011

My daughters—Sheena, Kayla, and Lori
My son Santos

The children I have raised as my
own—Addison and Dakota
And my granddaughter, Jeremy's daughter, Isabella (Bella)

CHAPTER 1

The Diagnosis

May 2011

I had been working for social services in the county for a few years. My job was working with child protection and children's mental health services. When a family was having problems, I would be assigned to work with them.

My goal was always to keep the family together. So I would meet with the families at their home and help with making referrals to services or sometimes helping the family deal with the issues they were having at the time. I was on the road traveling most of the week.

You worked a full-time job at a commercial building, sometimes working different shifts. You were also a single dad raising your beautiful two-year-old daughter. I would say, as a mother and son, we were close.

You talked to me about many things—some I wanted to hear and, at times, things I didn't want to hear. But you are my son. I would give my life for you.

I hope and pray that if anything in this life, you know how much I love you.

You had been complaining of your legs hurting, and lately, you had some stomach pains. I know you had seen several doctors but never seemed to get any answers for what was wrong.

This was the same thing you always heard. So I was guilty of not taking your pain very seriously.

But today was different. You were seeing a new doctor in Crookston. Your girlfriend Seneca was going with you today to your appointment. You had promised to call when you got home.

I was just finishing up with my last client for the day when you called. I excused myself and walked to the car to begin my drive home. You had a sense of urgency in your voice— something I had never heard before.

"Mom, I need you to come to the hospital." I asked, "What was wrong?"

I remember there were no tears, just the sound of you needing me as you said, "Things don't look so good. The doctor isn't letting me go home."

I just said okay and hung up the phone.

My mind was in a whirlwind, so many questions with no answers.

I continued down the road, maybe fifteen minutes to my office, not saying anything to anyone as I walked by numerous desks.

I passed my office and went to my friend Holly. She was the levelheaded friend who always took time to listen if I need a shoulder to lean on.

Holly asked what was going on, and I told her about our phone call. She knew you very well, and after listening to the crazy thoughts and ideas going through my head, I asked her what she thought could be going on when the doctor didn't want you to leave the hospital.

"Val, this is Jeremy we are talking about. Don't make a mountain out of a molehill."

Yep, she was right. I shouldn't worry about something if I don't know what it was.

I had a forty-five-mile drive to get to the hospital. My mind tried to think of what could possibly be wrong with a stomachache. Then I thought of gallstones. Everyone in my family has had them. Things would be fine.

I tried to recall through the years how many times you had been in the hospital. Once when you were three and had to have tubes put in your ears.

Jeremy, you have been the healthiest kid ever, not even a broken bone or a cavity for that matter. I bet you are scared.

Once I reached the hospital, I found the elevator and went to the third floor.

I arrived at the nurses' station and was instructed to walk to the end of the hall. What a long hallway that was.

You told me about a large blood clot going from your heart to below your stomach into your groin. This blood clot was affecting your heart, liver, and lungs.

The doctor had also identified three masses on your liver ranging from three centimeters to ten centimeters. They could be talking about cancer.

A biopsy was scheduled for Tuesday, but first, the doctors were going to try to see if they could dissolve the blood clot. You had started taking Coumadin to help with the blood clot. This was the first week of the rest of your life!

The next day was a Saturday. I was up early and took off to go see you again. I had spent Friday night calling and talking with family, letting everyone know what was going on. Of course I feel like I didn't know much, but just saying it may be cancer was very scary for me.

At this time, we had no idea what kind of cancer or if this was going to be something that the medical field had answers for. I was going to remain strong. I would not jump to any conclusions. I would believe!

You were in such good spirits today and talked about being bored and hungry.

Seneca and Bella were with you today. It sounded like Seneca was making plans with her parents to take Bella for a while until you were done with the doctor appointments.

I left Crookston in the late afternoon and headed for home. While I was driving, I received a call from my mom. She called to tell me that my dad had a stroke. The ambulance had been called, and he was now being airlifted to Fargo.

I remember the road becoming a blur from the tears. My heart was breaking in so many pieces. The man I considered my hero was struggling for his life.

My son, who would become my hero, was unaware of struggles he would be facing. I was now stuck, trying to decide if I should turn around and drive to spend time with my dad, or do I stay here for my son?

I returned another call to my mom when I got home. She did not think that I would need to drive to Fargo. She said they had been running tests on my dad, and so far, the doctors were not sure what was going on with him.

So I talked with my husband, Denny, and decided to stay home for you. The next day, I was told my dad was going to be released and sent home. He would have a follow-up appointment in Bemidji at Virginia.

On Monday, the Coumadin was stopped prior to the biopsy. On Tuesday morning, you were taken to Grand Forks hospital by ambulance. Your dad, Kevin; Seneca; and I drove to the hospital.

I can't say this was a fun day. Waiting is not something I am very good at. I have always said I have no patience. But we had to wait to see you until after everything was over.

This was one of those times when you said you had been in pain. The biopsy was done on your liver after you were returned to the hospital to readdress your medications. The doctor was not happy with the results of the Coumadin.

I think we were all starting to go crazy with the hospital stay. You kept telling me you didn't feel sick and just wanted to go home.

Seneca stayed with you at the hospital. Her parents had been so helpful by taking Bella home with them.

Denny and I made trips back to the hospital every day. By this time, the word *cancer* had become something we were getting used to hearing, but I was not sure any of us understood what this means or what we will be facing in the next few days, months, or even years.

This was just a mystery to us. The results of the biopsy confirmed the cancer. We were told it was fibrolamellar hepatocellular carcinoma.

Like that had any meaning to us. The doctor told us that your type of cancer makes the cell look like another cell is inside of it. Thanks to computers, we could look up information.

We discovered that it is a rare form of liver cancer that usually occurs in young adults who have no history of liver disease.

Each year, approximately two hundred people are diagnosed with this cancer worldwide. Patients typically present with a palpable abdominal mass but no symptoms. Although pain, weight loss, and jaundice may occur.

I didn't like what I found. I thought how a kid who had never been sick could get something so rare.

I remember talking to my friend Linda. She was going to school to become a nurse at the time. I explained what the doctor had said and what I knew so far. Right away, she started to look up whatever information she could find.

She called me back later that day, crying. I was scared to talk to her because I didn't want to hear what she was going to tell me.

She said the information she read stated that most people only live five years. All I could think was no one can put a time limit on the life of my son. We needed more answers. Going to the Mayo Clinic in Rochester may give us more answers. At this point, I had hope that things were going to change. Unbeknownst to me, the doctors found the cancer too late.

During this time, I was still trying to work as many hours as I could, trying to fit in work, hospitals, taking care of my family, and keeping people up-to-date on what news we were hearing.

I found a note I had sent to one of my friends. It read, "It's hard to work and think about the things that need to be taken care of, but I think work helps remind me that life is still normal for everyone else."

Jeremy had his appointment today with a county financial worker about insurance. Then I thought he was going to try to go to St. Cloud to spend time with Bella before going to Mayo Clinic this weekend.

He had blood work done yesterday, and some of the results were not what we expected. I thought it was with the blood thinner. It was not doing the job they expected. Then he got home and ended up back at the ER.

He had been throwing up all day and could not even keep water down. So they gave him an IV and sent him home.

I decided that I was not going with him because if the news was something worse again, I don't know that I could handle it all.

We were leaving on Sunday for Rochester and would be back on Tuesday. Jeremy and Seneca would stay down there until they were done with the tests. Sounds like it would be three to five days. I would go down there again if it is decided they are going to do surgery.

But at this time, we didn't know what was going on. I just wanted them to take it out of him.

Each day, knowing cancer had the chance to grow more scared me. I felt like I was running a race, my stomach hurt so bad, and I was being forced to finish the race when all I wanted to do was to laid down and stop running.

I didn't want to finish this race. I was scared of the nights and days that I have in the future when I won't be able to hold everything together anymore. I couldn't believe I was even able to admit this.

You were able to spend a couple of days home before going to Rochester. I felt bad because Bella was not home to enjoy this time with you. I was so thankful you were able to leave a few days early to spend some time with her.

Bella was still staying with Seneca's parents. Those few days at home went by so fast.

I remember thinking once we went to Mayo, the doctors would do surgery or chemo. I wasn't sure what, but I was looking for answers, and I believed we would have them. I really couldn't explain how I was feeling during this first week.

Hearing the word *cancer* was like someone shooting a gun at you just to get your attention. So okay, you have my attention. Why couldn't this happen to someone who was on drugs or drinking or anyone else but my son? This was the little boy I had twenty-four years ago. He had always been healthy—the one who could make me so mad and then turn around and make me laugh over something dumb.

A single dad raising his two-year-old daughter, he worked hard, loved the Lord, brought Bella to church every chance he had. All he wanted out of life right now was to be a good dad.

Bella needed her daddy. I needed my son.

Please, dear God, don't let anything happen to him. I need answers, and I want them now. I just want everything to go back to normal and be okay.

June 6, 2011

Well, we had our first day at Mayo Clinic. My heart was still very hopeful, and we were able to have good conversations and joke about things.

Jeremy, you were so upset because your motel room had mold around the shower, and you were worried that this will make you sick. You reminded me that you already had cancer.

We joked about giving blood, how each person was called up to the desk, taken into the back, and came out with a colored bandage, like they were all being given some secret drug.

Our first experience at Mayo Clinic was very different from what we were used to. I think it is nice to have the same doctor year after year who knows you well. But when you get to a big place like this, you are not familiar with anyone. You become just a number to these doctors.

So we walked so much to different places—an area for blood work, one for X-rays, CT scans, and MRIs. So strange compared to our small-town experiences.

I don't want to say I was naive, but I guess I just hadn't thought about the reality of what was going on with you.

Seneca and I both had a conversation about the news we had been told today. Up to now, we knew the cancer was in your blood. That was the reason you have this large blood clot.

I had not thought about how the blood was traveling around your body and spreading the cancer. The doctors took the time to show us the scan of your liver today, which had a dark cloud in the middle of it.

This was the big mass. It was not on the surface of your liver, but it was inside. They said your liver was very large, which was pushing all your organs into your stomach.

This was the reason you were in so much pain and uncomfortable. You hadn't eaten anything in the last couple of days, but you had gained five pounds. Remember how they had scales in the halls of the clinic, and you would stop to weigh yourself every time we walked by one.

I look at you, Jeremy, with such love. I still see my little boy with the beautiful blue eyes and blond hair. What a precious gift from God you are! I see those beautiful eyelashes, and I think they haven't changed in all the years since I first held you—the day you were born you never even cried.

You took your first breath and just lay in the little bed looking around, trying to figure out your new world.

I had a perfect little boy. You grew up to have deep blue eyes that sparkled when you smiled and a laugh that was so silly it made others laugh just to hear it. I know you get your sense of humor from me, although yours is twisted at times.

I love the way you love your daughter. You amaze me! Your thoughts are with your friends and family, always trying to help others or come up with a crazy plan to make yourself rich.

June 7, 2011

It was two thirty in the morning. Your birthday was in a couple of days on June 10. I was still not sure what we would do for your special day.

I would love to have a surprise party for you, but it was so hard to plan right now when we were so far away from home.

During this last week when we had been gone, I had been on the phone with your sister Kayla, and we had been making plans. So the idea was that there was going to be a garage sale to try to help out with the cost of the motels and you not being able to work. I think Kayla and my friends did most of the work to get the word out.

They had people donating items to be sold. Since we were at the hospital, we were not able to work with the sale. Kayla came home from college and stayed at the house.

I remember getting calls and Kayla asking me if I really need things in the house, she was putting stuff on the sale. They were going to do things a little bit differently with this sale.

We did not have time to plan for the sale, and we did not know what items would be delivered.

The girls were going to have a donation sale, and people could just make an offer on the items they wish to buy.

I prayed for you so much tonight, thanking God for the chance to be in such a wonderful hospital with doctors here who had so much wisdom. I thanked God for giving us peace and the answers to insurance. We were so blessed!

I prayed that God would allow you to just go to the bathroom so you wouldn't feel so much pressure and pain. You had been complaining about more stomach pains in the last couple of days, telling me your stomach was hurting because you hadn't gone to the bathroom since we left home.

I knew you're hurt, and I couldn't take the pain away.

My heart hurt for you.

I thanked God for giving you medication to help with the pain. He is a wonderful god. I was thinking tonight if you get to heaven before I do, God could have Grandpa watch over you.

I remember how you sat by my grandpa Lester's bed every day when he was sick. I was now praying that God would just give me peace and help me to accept the future as part of his plan. I felt like I was so weak, and yet everyone expected me to be strong. I was not sure I could do this. Yet you didn't give up. I could never tell you enough how much I love you!

My husband Denny and I came back to Fosston on Tuesday night of June 8. Your dad Kevin and his wife Karen went to Rochester to be with you while we were home. I tried to go to work that Wednesday, but that didn't happen.

I couldn't stay at work. I couldn't stop crying, and each time I was asked about you, the tears fell from my eyes.

I had no control over my tears. Was this grief or just the love of a mother who was scared?

I had no idea what these feelings were. But I knew it didn't mix well with my work.

So I called my boss Molly to say I was home and was going to try to work a couple of days. She said she wanted to talk to me, and she was coming to Fosston. She asked if we could meet at my house.

She came over, and the first thing she asked me was why was I going to work when you were still at the hospital. She told me to pack my bags and get back down there to be with you. I was so glad she made me do that. I ended up taking time off work until I could go back and do my duties for others.

Seneca called on Wednesday night to tell me that Thursday, June 9, they might do surgery on you. I was so excited to hear that something was going to be done.

Our friend Jen wanted to go to see you. I knew her car would not make the trip, so I asked her to come with me. Denny may have to come home earlier to return to work, so Jennifer would ride with me, and Denny would drive in his pickup. I won't have to be alone. I washed two loads of clothes, repacked the suitcase, and we headed out to Rochester again.

We decided to stop in the cities to spend the night. It was getting too late, and I didn't know if we could find a place to stay once we got to Rochester.

We had a difficult time finding a motel. It didn't matter. I knew God would provide something for us.

We finally found a place around midnight on the east side of the cities. The new plan was to get up early and get to the hospital by 8:00 a.m.

The next morning, I don't remember what time we got up and started driving, but I know we were not going to make it to the hospital by eight in the morning.

You called while I was driving. You wanted to know where I was and when I would get there. I asked what the plan was, and you told me you weren't sure, but you had just finished breakfast.

Right away, I knew something was wrong. If you were eating breakfast, I knew you wouldn't be having surgery.

I remember waiting in the hallway while speaking to my mom on the phone that day. I looked into the room off to the left of your room. Inside was a young guy who was bald.

The thought came to my head for the first time: *Is that what we have to look forward to?*

We had been told that there would be no surgery today. The doctor would be in soon to talk to us. Seneca, Denny, Jen, and I all stood around and just waited.

It was early afternoon before the doctor came into the room. That was when we heard the devastating news.

Do you ever feel like you are in a movie?

Time stands still, and you are able to see the look on everyone's face and feel the emotions in the air. How can the words of one person change your world forever? They can kill all your hopes and dreams and take away everything you have been holding on to in just minutes.

Here, this little petite female doctor trying to stand tall and give us an update on what was going on. But she couldn't look at us, and tears were falling down her cheeks. We were all fixed on her and the words she had to say.

All was quiet.

She said they had planned on replacing the vein going from your heart to your kidneys. However, they were unable to. We were told that the cancer was causing the blood to clot in more places now.

There was another spot above your kidneys and a tumor was in your heart. Your body had suffered too much damage, and they couldn't fix it. She said she would advise us to go home and call hospice. My mind was just stuck on the word *damage* and not fixable.

I remember the quiet. You sat up in the bed, Seneca was with you, I stood at the end of the bed, and Denny and Jen were standing by the door. All eyes were fixed on the doctor.

I was sure we were all thinking the same thing, but I finally asked how long. She looked down and opened her arms as if she didn't have a true answer. I heard two weeks to a couple of months.

Denny and Jen left the room. Seneca, you, and I huddled on the bed; and we cried. I wanted to take away everything the doctor said. I wanted to be alone with you, hold you, and tell you everything was going to be okay. But the damage was done; the words were spoken. This was the beginning of a long journey no one wants to take.

Seneca wanted to try to find another hospital, maybe to see if something more could be done. I wanted to take you home and just hold you. I thought if you only have a short time left, I wanted it to be with family and people you love, not running from doctor to doctor. We all decided to go home.

Phone calls started. I don't know what happened or how people knew. I think I called my parents to let them know the doctors were not going to do surgery.

I must have told my mom, you may only have a couple of weeks to live. I really didn't remember. I know I ended up telling this story so many times, but I don't remember who to or what was said. I don't even remember if we ate that afternoon.

Tomorrow was your twenty-fifth birthday, and what would it be like? I just wanted to leave, get out of this hospital, and process this new information.

You and Seneca waited at the hospital for the discharge paperwork. Denny, Jen, and I decided to take off for home.

You were going to stop in St. Cloud and spend the night there with Bella before heading home in the morning.

I just wanted to go home. I don't know how I was ever going to make it through this. Parents were not supposed to watch their children suffer and die.

Jen and I were driving down the road headed west toward the cities, and every once in a while, we looked back to see Denny following behind us in his little pickup.

This trip was not going as I had thought. No good reports from the medical staff, no exciting plans for Jeremy's birthday. At this point, what more could possible happen? We were outside a small town only a few miles from Rochester, and we noticed that Denny was no longer following behind us.

We turned around and went a couple of miles and found Denny on the side of the road; his pickup was broken down. Jen had roadside assistance on her phone, so we were able to get help quickly.

After about an hour of waiting, we returned to this small town.

The pickup was towed to a garage, where the guy promised to have it fixed early the next morning. We followed him back and paid for the towing fee.

I remember this was the first time I told someone about your cancer face-to-face. I explained to the service guy that we had just left the hospital with the news my son was dying. He said he was sorry and would get right to work on the truck. We found a motel close by and prepared to spend the night.

I think this had to have been one of the craziest days I have ever lived. Not one thing seemed to go our way.

Kayla had called to tell me about the garage sale and how the plans were going. She said my dog Shaggy was sick, really sick and would need to get to the vet hopefully tomorrow.

You had called once we got to the motel to tell me that Seneca had locked the keys in her car. You had stopped for as at some rest stop.

I just couldn't think of how I was going to go and help you out. But shortly after, you called and said she found the keys in the bathroom on a hook. What a crazy day that was.

Jen had looked at me, shaking her head and said she doesn't want to live my life.

I know I didn't sleep much. Listening to Denny snore and hearing Jen breathing, my mind just wouldn't shut down.

On Friday morning around eight thirty, the pickup was fixed. Another $170, and we are on the road again.

Your dad and Karen had started to drive down on Thursday, but when they got the information that you were being discharged, they decided to stay home.

Kayla and my friends had the garage sale going. Kayla was telling me how people had donated furniture, clothes, baked goods, and all kinds of items for the sale today. Since there wasn't time to mark prices on the items, we decided to make it a Name Your Price sale. Kayla said that the little old ladies attending the garage sale did not like to name their own price.

I kept getting calls asking about furniture in the house and items I had if I would mind having them on the sale. Secretly I think this was Kayla's chance to get rid of some of the items I hung on to and didn't really need. I couldn't believe the friends and family who had given of their time to help. We are so blessed.

After sharing with so many families the news we had received from the hospital and knowing it was your birthday, I can say it was a mutual decision with everyone to have a surprise birthday party for you on Sunday.

Today was Saturday, your birthday. I won't even get to spend the day with you.

Your aunt Tammy was on her way home from Kentucky. She would be flying in this afternoon. I also was told your uncle Kenny would be coming home from South Dakota. Wow, I can't even express the feelings I had.

We decided to invite everyone from our Facebook contacts. Since it was only announced on Friday, I was not sure how many people would attend on Sunday. It was not a lot of notice, but it was the best we could do.

How do you plan the last birthday your child will ever have? I guess it is hard to even think about it that way.

I was busy looking for pictures of you. I wanted them all on the wall in the kitchen so people can see the joy you have brought to everyone for the last twenty-five years.

I know it isn't normal, but to make sure we have enough food, I asked for a potluck if everyone brings something we should have plenty to eat.

Jeremy, your birthday will be remembered by many! We had over one hundred people at the house—relatives from your dad's family, my family, and so many friends. People just kept stopping by all day long. We had plenty of food!

Pastor Strenge from the Baptist Church came to your birthday as well. You had gone into the back bedroom to lay down for a while.

During that time, Grandma DeeDee asked Pastor if he would pray for you. So Grandpa Leif, Grandma DeeDee, Uncle Obie, Aunt Janie, Great-grandma Bergeson, your cousin Jesse, Aunt Tammy, Seneca, Kayla, and your dad Kevin all came in the room to pray for you.

Pastor anointed you with oil and said a prayer. Everyone took turns praying for you.

This was such a special time, almost a feeling of everyone being of one spirit. This was hard to explain, but it was a time of realizing that God had given me a son, and he knew what was best for you.

I will let you go if he calls you to heaven, but I know my heart will break. I know that if you are healed, you will amaze many with your story.

Either way, I think God has something amazing planned for the future. I don't know what it is or when it will happen, but it will be a miracle.

By the end of our little prayer group, everyone was crying. We didn't have any Kleenex in the room, so Kayla ran across the hall and grabbed toilet paper out of the bathroom. It worked, and we were all able to share. I think we had company at the house till after ten that night.

Oh, Jeremy, my hope and prayer is that someday you will be able to read this journal and see how many people have shown their love and support for you. How, as a mom, I always and forever see you as my little boy. Doesn't matter how big you get to be. I have loved you from the first day I knew you began to form. A mother does not stop loving!

I was getting so tired. All I wanted to do was sleep. But nighttime was not good. Everything was quiet, and all my head wanted to do was remember my little boy. I thought about that sweet soft voice that you have when you call my name. I thought about you and your sisters and how you all grew up so fast. If I could go back to the days when you were all little, I wouldn't have to think about losing you. I didn't think I would even get mad at you now for driving the lawn mower into the garage door.

Up to now, we had had a very busy couple of weeks. The only time to really think about things was when I was supposed to be sleeping.

I already told you had that was working out, so Monday was coming in the morning. We don't really know it yet, but it was the start of a new way of life for us.

On Monday, I went to the see chiropractor. It felt good to have some work done on the sore back.

I made him cry when I told him about you being sick and what was going on. I didn't mean to tell him, but stress had a way of making me emotional.

My next appointment was with the doctor I always see at the clinic. I needed to know if she could help me get some sleep.

That appointment went well. I made her cry too. Then I made the nurse cry. Next was to pick up medications and head off to Crookston for your doctor appointment.

I don't remember if your doctor had any information from Mayo Clinic yet, but it seems he didn't.

So he was filled in with what we knew. You had your list of things you needed to talk about. Your legs were starting to swell already, and at times, it was painful for you to walk.

You wanted to know how you could get a wheelchair and a handicap sticker for your car. The last thing we talked about was hospice.

This program may be great for some people, but I don't think right now it was the right thing for us. You were not ready to throw in the towel and say you are going to die.

Hospice to you means you were admitting the end. No, thank you. We could stick with doctor appointments for now.

During the first couple of weeks home, we had a change in our relationship. It was hard to describe, but it was different. You would come to the house in the morning to have coffee with me.

Oh, you will never know how much I enjoyed that time with you even the times you feel asleep holding your coffee.

During these morning visits, you would usually take out your container of pills. Some were before you eat, and other you had with food.

I am just surprised you can keep this straight in your mind. One morning, aunties Kelly and Tammy came over for coffee with us before they went back to their homes. It was always so nice to be able to just really sit down and enjoy the company and time with people.

I remember I once attended a training for work, and the speaker talked about the love gifts. I had never heard of this before and didn't know what he was talking about. But now this is all starting to make sense to me, and I see and understand what a love gift is. He said there are five gifts:

(1) spending time with someone,
(2) giving gifts,

(3) doing something for someone,

(4) saying the words "I love you," and

(5) showing affection like a hug.

He explained how people need to receive some of or maybe all the gifts to feel love.

Some people know how to give some of the gifts but may not know how to give them all. I don't know if this will make sense to everyone, but it opened my eyes. I understand the gift of doing something for someone or just spending time with them. It is love gifts we are seeing so much of right now.

People are saying I love you and giving a hug. I wonder if they know how important it is to share these gifts and to receive them as well.

Our week was going by so quickly, and you had decided to make some changes.

You and Seneca had planned to get married in September, but now with a time limit, the two of you had decided to get married in June.

Some of our friends had come together and decided that they were going to put on a benefit supper to help with raising money.

I was feeling like I was under pressure so much to do and not sure if we have time. The money from the benefit needed to go into an account at the bank, and we needed to have someone in charge of the money.

You thought I should do this. The plan right now was that this money would be used to help with living expenses since you were unable to work.

Do you remember when you were around twelve years old? Kevin and I decided to do foster care. We got Santos and Lori that year.

Santos was nine and full of piss and vinegar, and Lori was only seventeen months old. It took five years for the adoption to go through so that they could have a forever home. That could be another story.

This afternoon, my friend Holly was coming over to pick up Lori and take her to her place. I went to the bank to open an account for the benefit. We also had the chance to speak with a nurse from hospice. They would need to talk to the doctor. I decided to have a bonfire tonight and just sit down and relax. Maybe it would clear my head.

Seneca had been so busy taking care of you and working on the wedding, which was only a week away.

You and Seneca had a good part of things already planned and talked about, so I was sure it makes things easier for her. But I couldn't imagine how stressed she must be.

Having a wedding will be a good distraction for us. No cancer thoughts just what made you happy.

I had a very odd phone call today. Some guy called. He said he had spoken with my brother Tony.

Tony told this guy about you and your cancer. It reminded me later to tell your uncle not to give my number out to strangers.

This guy kept me on the phone for about twenty minutes. He wanted to talk to me about how much God loves us, and how he is able to do miracles. I had no problem listening to that part of the conversation. But I was not comfortable with some of the things he was saying.

I listened to him and tried to share my opinions, but he had different ideas. He told me that he believes you will not die, but you will be asleep in Christ. I am not sure I understand exactly what he is talking about. But in my mind, if this is true, you will be cold in a casket in the ground.

I chose to believe that if you die, Jesus will be waiting to take you to heaven. You will not suffer, and you will be made perfect.

Remember how we read that book about that little boy dying and going to heaven? I want to believe that is what it will be like.

Our body is just a shell holding our soul. When we die, the body remains, and the soul goes to heaven or hell. You had a doctor appointment today in Crookston.

They were going to try to get some fluid drained.

Kayla just called to let me know they had gotten two liters of fluid removed. I sure hope you were feeling better now, and I couldn't wait to see you when you get home.

June 17, 2011

Tomorrow was your wedding. So today we had been very busy getting last minute things done, and tonight we were working on decorations for the reception.

We had a good number of people at the reception sight, helping to get tables set up, and the decorating done. It turned out to be an awkward night.

Bella was running around and having so much fun playing with balloons and kicking them around the floor. At one point, I turned around, and there was Jessica, Bella's mother. She hadn't even tried to see Bella in months, and now suddenly here she was.

Bella had her second birthday in March. Jessica showed up with a birthday gift for her three months later.

I don't think anyone knew how to respond or what to say. I tried to hide the uncomfortable feeling and just be friendly.

I was not the one who had made the decision about Bella's care or who had custody of her. I just knew as a mom. I would see my child even if it meant going to the other person's house for that visit.

Bella was excited about the little doll in a stroller, and it kept her entertained throughout the evening. Jessica informed me that she planned to attend the benefit as well.

June 18, 2011

No wedding ever goes perfect, right?

Seneca had worked very hard to pull everything together. She had a beautiful dress and had Bella looking like a little angel.

I found the day to be rather stressful. We had someone who could play the piano for Seneca's entrance, but she wanted a certain song from a CD played.

Well, we didn't have anyone to run the sound system in the church. So I found a cousin of mine and asked him if he knew how to work the sound system. He went back in the room and played around with the CD until he got it working.

Next big thing for me was getting someone to usher the grandparents and mothers up to the front. My thought was that Seneca would never know how many people I chased after and how many times I told someone what to do. But the day finally happened, and it turned out beautiful.

I don't know how many people attended the wedding. It seemed like the church was pretty full. I sure did enjoy looking at the video Denny took of the service.

Remember how Kayla and Grandma Baumann were standing next to you for a picture? Grandma kept leaning over and kissing your ear and neck. I sure hope we got pictures someplace of that.

I know we all got a good laugh out of it. I had not expected you and Seneca to give your mothers flowers.

Seneca walked to her parents and presented her mother with a flower. She leaned over to kiss her dad, and I was guessing she told them she loved them.

You walked over to me, your hand on your cane to keep your balance. I didn't know should I stand or stay seated in my chair.

I was crying and didn't want anyone to see. You reached down to hug me, and I didn't want to let go. It seems like those seconds or minutes could last forever.

I could hear people behind me and all over the church crying. It was such a touching moment.

You turned and walked back up to the pastor. Someone must have reminded you to go over and hug your dad. He was standing up for you. So there was a little chuckle from the audience, and you walked over to hug him.

The people attending the wedding as guests were there to show you their love.

You had the reception in Fosston. That was also a very difficult thing for me. I watched you dance, and no matter how long you had been on your feet, you still got up to enjoy the day.

I cried when you held Bella in your arms and danced to the song "I Loved Her First." I wonder if you will ever dance with her again.

We both cried to the mother-and-son song "Forever Young." In my mind, you would always be young and full of energy.

I could not finish the dance with you. It was very hard for both of us. We cried; you kissed me and told me you loved me. I can never tell you enough how much I love you.

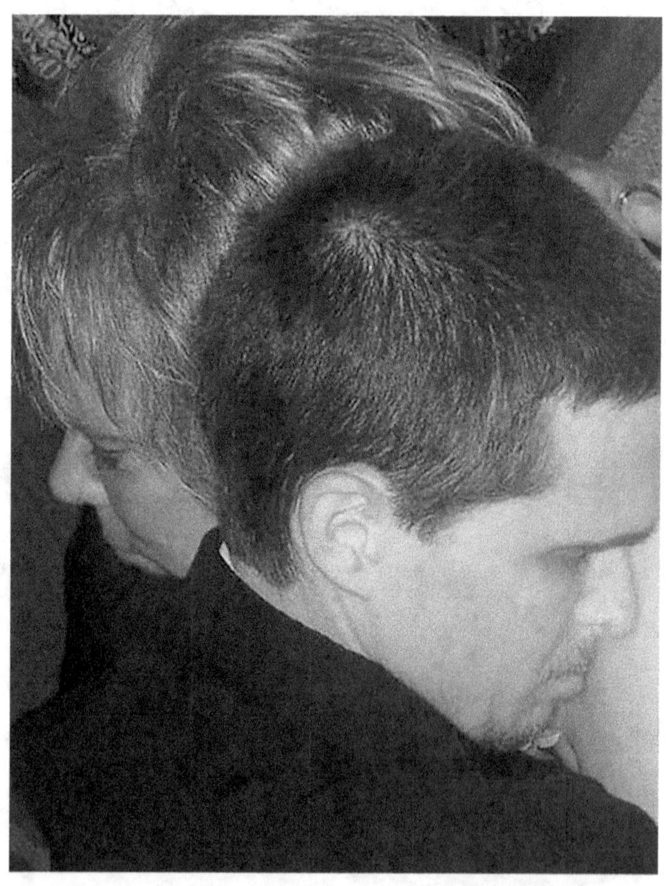

During the day, we had several good times to cry, and it didn't matter that people watched, or that pictures were taken.

My favorite pictures of your wedding day were of you hugging your momma and the one of you dancing with Bella. For a moment, we held each other close, and I wanted time to stand still. I didn't want to let our hug end. I worried for you all day today. Your color was not good, and your legs were so swollen by the end of the day.

People noticed. I said nothing. I had already gotten use to saying nothing about how you feel. You got upset if people know the truth, so I said you were doing fine.

I am sure there was a picture of you sitting in your wheelchair while Kayla was rubbing your feet. I wonder how long you would have with your new family.

After the wedding, I came home and got your pictures online. I couldn't wait to see them. Kayla spent the night at the house, and I think she was going to be home till the benefit now.

This, by the way, was coming along great. People were dropping things off at the house almost daily. Baskets of items for the silent auction were piling up in the entry.

June 19, 2011

The doctor had started you on a new medication to help with the blood clots. You would now be getting Lovenox shots twice a day in your belly. It must be working as the swelling in your legs seemed to have gone down.

It was so good to see you being able to move around so much easier. I had read that the medication would also give you more energy. I am sure you had not read up on it because you didn't seem to notice the help the medication was giving you. You called to tell me you could jump once in the air. You were so happy.

At times, it was really difficult for me. You continued to deny that you were sick, and when the medications were working and you felt better, you said that you were healed.

The medication was helping with the blood clots, so you had increased circulation and improved energy.

Honey, that is not taking away the tumors in your heart and in your liver. But I will not take away your hope.

We found out that hospice would not be working with you at this time. The reason being is that you were taking this new medication for the blood clots. They considered Lovenox as a treatment, and they would not work with people who are getting treatment. Not to mention the cost of the medication, if you have hospice, they will not pay for you to be on this medication.

I think your words had something to do with your not dying, and their job was to work with people who are dying. I believe without this medication, you are going to die, and I want you here with us for as long as we can have you!

I don't know if mood changes are coming with the medications, you are on or what. You seem to get angry so quickly.

It hurt so bad when you were like that. I was always afraid I was going to say the wrong thing or do something wrong. I didn't want to get you upset. I only wanted the best for you and try to do things to help. At times, it made me feel like such a bad mom.

I continued to have a difficult time sleeping at nights. I had times when I fall asleep, but I had such crazy dreams. Last night was really hard for me. I had a dream you were found dead. I had to identify you by your class ring. Do you remember when we picked out that ring? You wanted something different and chose a ring with two birthstones. You wanted your birthstone and mine on the ring. I wonder how many young guys would do that for their moms.

I now wore that ring every day. One day, it will belong to Bella.

I was up once again from 1:30 a.m. to 3:00 a.m. I am not sure if little to no sleep was normal for a mom or not. I so wanted my life and the things we do to be back to normal.

This was not normal! We now counted pills and made sure you get your shots twice a day, always making sure to give the shots on opposite sides of your tummy. Seneca and I were giving you the shots.

June 29, 2011

Today was June 29. It was your cousin Jesse's birthday. Our normal routine would be to go and celebrate his birthday with family. But we didn't do normal anymore. I was just in amazement on how six weeks had changed our lives: from hearing the word *cancer*, having the diagnosis, and trips to the doctor, Rochester, and ER a couple of times.

We had a garage sale, a wedding, and now a benefit coming up—didn't matter none of it. You were still alive, and we had passed a deadline. Keep fighting, Jeremy. You have so much to live for.

You and Seneca had decided to get away for a family trip. I remember thinking would this be your last trip with Bella? Would you be able to do things with her as she gets older? What would she remember?

I know you went to the cities and took Bella to the zoo and the underwater aquarium. When you were at her parents, you went to take time to go fishing and motorbike riding. I think you were having a good time.

Until you called on a Monday night saying you were having stomach pains. It was so hard for me not to be close to you when you are sick.

My heart just broke. You said you went Monday night, all day Tuesday in pain until you went to the doctor in St. Cloud on Tuesday night. The doctor there said it was some gastric stuff going on, so they gave you some medication and sent you home. I want you home here so that I can see you. It was so hard for a mom when she can't help make her child feel better.

We had your benefit, and it went so well. I can't even express the love and support I felt. I hope you felt the same way.

I remember it was a day you were feeling really good, and you said if you didn't sit in your wheelchair, people wouldn't believe you were sick. You were such a dork at times, but that was just another part of your personality we loved so much.

Our friends Rocksanne, Wendie, Donna, and Jen worked so hard to get everything set up. We think it was over two hundred people there.

Do you know how much you are loved? People mad up around forty baskets which were auctioned off and some that were raffled. I think we have enough hot dogs, buns, ketchup, and mustard to last close to a year.

I spent some time with my mom and dad over the weekend. Grandpa Leif was having such a difficult time dealing with you being sick.

It was such an eye-opener because I think we stayed busy and had so many things going on all the time. I seldom had time to realize how your illness was causing pain to others around us as well.

I cried when my dad told me that he felt like a part of him was dying. I didn't like to talk about cancer. I didn't like to see my dad cry or hurt.

This road we were walking on was so difficult. The days you felt good, I was scared because I did not know what would be next.

When you got sick, it seemed like symptoms happen so fast and without warning.

I tried to thank God every day for the little things. I hope you were doing the same. But on the other side, I would admit, it was hard for me to see some people walking around healthy when I know they are doing things daily to damage their bodies.

You had your whole life ahead of you and a little girl who needed you. I just wanted you to know as of right now, I wanted you home so I could be close to you.

I love talking to you on the phone every day just to hear what you were doing. I love how you told me you love me. I was so going to miss the sound of your voice and the sound of you love. I felt like we were in a dream. None of this was real, and one day, I would wake up and know this was just a nightmare.

Your sister Sheena had her birthday on June 23. I went over to her house to bring her a birthday cake. It was so hard to see your place right next door and knowing you were not home. I wonder if you remembered to call her.

Having the two of you live so close together was nice. I know she could just yell out her window, and you could see her.

You called and said that during your vacation, you had been able to do much of the walking. Sounds like you were still enjoying your vacation.

You only used your wheelchair while you were at the zoo. Almost like God knew you needed that time of feeling better. What a memory you had made for your wife and daughter this week.

I was happy to see you when you returned home on July 5. Best part you are still alive and fighting every day to beat this cancer. I wanted to see you so bad; my heart ached. I returned to work on July 6. I stopped by your house that morning basically to tell you that I loved you. Both you and Seneca talked with me. We laughed and talked about the plans for the week.

I went over to the office to start my day and catch up on the work I had missed. I was there for about an hour when you called to tell me I needed to hurry to the house.

When I arrived, I just walked in. You had swelling in your head on the right temple. It was so surprising because I had just left. Where did this come from, and what is it?

It was actually funny to see this big bulge on the side of your forehead. You and I both laughed at it. But deep down, we all knew we needed to go to the hospital to find out what was going on. I prayed it was not a blood clot or another tumor forming in your head. This happened so fast.

I called my boss and let her know we had to take off for the clinic because we were concerned you may have another blood clot.

We went to Crookston, and they did a CT scan right away. I can't remember what you called it, but I know you referred to something from Star Wars. Saying you had a baseball in your head pretty much describes the way it looked.

After we got back home, you went to Bagley to spend some time with your dad. I think you just wanted to show off your new look.

We did not hear until five thirty that evening that this was most likely another blood clot. You were put on a steroid and just had to wait.

The next day, the swelling had gone down just as quickly as it had appeared. We went back to the doctor on June 11. Your dad, aunt, and Karen had you so stressed out thinking you would die from this blood clot. But I believe it would go away, and you would be fine. It was not in your brain; it was on the outside of your skull.

July 11, 2011

We returned to the doctor for your appointment. It was a very difficult day for you.

Another CT scan at eight thirty in the morning. We had to meet with the doctor at eleven thirty for the results. We talked with the doctor about the swelling in your feet. He said that your liver was almost completely shut down. Your body was not producing the proteins in needs to work correctly.

I asked him if it would help being on a high protein diet. His words cut deep as he told us *nothing* was going to help. He said the best thing for you is to do whatever makes you happy.

I mentioned the diet Seneca had you on to be healthier. Again, he said it won't make any difference. He told you this with tears in his own eyes. He said if he had a magic wand, he would wave it and make you better.

But even with a new liver, it would do no good. In desperation, I told him how well you have been doing. I talked about the wheelchair, the cane, and how you could walk on your own and the energy you had.

He bowed his head slightly and told us this was part of the pattern. The name for it was *rally*. He said when patients are told they are dying, their bodies fight back with energy at times making them feel so good.

Many people believe during this time that they no longer are sick. But he said it never lasts for long. Eventually, it would stop, and the weakness would reappear.

We talked about your heart as well. I asked the doctor if he knew how large the tumor was in your heart. He looked in your charts, then looked up at me to tell me it was two inches in diameter.

I lost so much hope at that time. It felt like I was being told again two weeks maybe longer if we are lucky.

I don't know what you and Seneca were feeling at that time. I was crying. I tried so hard to control the tears, but they fell anyway.

You were sitting on the examination table trying so hard to be brave and block out the words we had just heard. I could see the pain in your face.

I remember thinking you were sitting alone. I wanted to run to you, but it was a little room. So I walked over to you just to hold you tight.

I didn't even know what to say. You were so hurt, and I am sure you were afraid. But I know I won't hear the words, so I would not bring it up.

I thought a mom was able to do magic and kiss the hurts goodbye. This mom was all out of magic. All I had left was love and hugs. But it was never enough.

I needed to just stop, breath, and take a long look at my priorities—God, my family, and the families I work with. They are all so important to me, but in my mind, I know things have to change.

So I decided that I am not going to keep working every day. I just couldn't do this when I have no idea how long I have left with you.

You are my son, and to think that one day I will not have you in my life is killing me.

I can't imagine you not being here. Denny and I talked, and he thought we would be able to make it on half my paycheck.

I would have to talk with my boss. I had to get another note from the doctor to have the time off work.

Molly said they would be willing to let me go to half day. I was so relieved to know the pressure of work would be lifted.

July 13 was Denny's sixtieth birthday. We had a small party at the house.

Grandpa Leif and Grandma DeeDee came over along with Great-grandma Bergeson. Janie and Obie were here as well. Janet, Jen, and my friend Holly all stopped by to wish him a happy birthday. Denny's daughter Kim had called, and he sure did enjoy talking with her.

You, Seneca, and Bella came over later in the day. One day when things seemed kind of normal, what more could we ask for? I wondered how many times we will be able to have get-togethers like this.

Kayla started her internship in Grand Forks this week. She called every day to give me an update on how it was going for her.

I don't know where she got her energy. She was still trying to keep her other two jobs going as well as do the internship.

She said today that she was starting to get her headaches again. I worried about her taking on so much and still dealing with you being sick.

She worried about you all the time. Sometimes when we talked, she told me to not say anything about your health because she already knew. I felt like I had no one to talk to.

Truth is who can I talk to, and who will understand? You have Seneca, and to me, it seemed the two of you refused to talk about the reality of dying.

Denny is your stepdad, so I don't think he had the same parent feelings I have. Your dad talked to Karen if he talks at all. The girls didn't want to talk to me or hear what was going on. I talked to my friends, but I didn't dare say what I was really feeling. I didn't want to make those talks uncomfortable for anyone. Not sure what I would do if I couldn't pray.

I didn't want anyone to feel sorry for us or me. I just didn't like feeling alone and like no one understood. I wonder how people who don't believe in God can get through times like this.

Today you told me how weak you were feeling I want to blame it on something, anything. Maybe you weren't getting enough sleep. But you said you couldn't sleep you just feel like you need to do something. I didn't know then, but I know now, this was just the beginning of the anxiety. We planned to go tubing down the Red River this weekend. But you said you didn't feel strong enough, and neither of us wanted to take the risk of you drowning.

Jeremy, if I am hurting this bad on the inside, what are you feeling?

CHAPTER 2

Months to Say Goodbye

I got a card in the mail today from the ladies at the church. They were praying for strength and courage for us.

I didn't understand why people pray for me. It was my son who needed the strength and courage than I as the mom, and I think I was supposed to be strong.

I got another card in the mail today. It was full of encouragement. It said,

What Cancer Cannot Do

Cancer is so limited…
It cannot cripple love
It cannot shatter hope
It cannot corrode faith
It cannot eat away peace
It cannot destroy confidence

It cannot kill friendships
It cannot shut out memories
It cannot silence courage
It cannot reduce eternal life
It cannot quench the spirit
It cannot lessen the power of the resurrection!

August 2, 2011

I continued to have contact with my friends at work. They all seemed to really be concerned about you and wanted updates often.

Jeremy was doing really well. He looked better than he had in a long time. His feet were no longer swollen, and his stomach was down.

He was skinny and walked weird but was looking good. I had never been this close to someone with cancer, so I was not sure what to expect or what was normal.

He was still on morphine and took strong medication to hold his food down. He had been so temperamental. Other than that, he was good.

Doctors still would not do anything or run any tests. So we remained in the same waiting game—wait to get better or wait to die.

Looking back now, I see how I tried so hard to make things sound normal yet added a little detail to our reality. This is what our reality was: pretend things were good. But know they were falling apart, and we were lost, not knowing what to do.

So here we were almost in the middle of August. Wow, what a way we had spent the summer!

I ached to spend some time with you, took you out to eat, just you and me. But I know that was not going to happen.

I was becoming so angry at Seneca. I didn't want to be, but it was very difficult. A part of me felt like she was taking the last few months away from me that I should be spending with my son.

The last two weeks, you had spent angry at me. It was all because of the benefit money. Before even having the benefit, you had to decide what money was going to be used for.

You were the one who wanted me to handle the money. I put it in an account for you, and I was more than willing to hand over enough to pay your bills.

I did not ask to do this. Both you and Seneca did not seem to understand that the committee put me in charge of this after you named me to do it. For some reason, you thought after everything was over. I would hand all the money over to you.

I know you had always been the kind of person who wants things to go your way, and when they don't, you get mad. But what we went through at this time was way past that point.

I am not sure where it all started. I know you would tell Seneca one thing and tell me something different just to see if we would argue. But this time, Seneca had more to do with it.

You became so angry with me that you started to call all over town to tell people I had stolen your money.

You called the benefit office, and then you called the cops, trying to get me arrested for theft. What made it more difficult was you even called your sisters and other family members to tell you called the cops. You would never know how much you and Seneca had hurt me. But I know you were sick, and I was not going to let this control how I felt.

Then we had the issue of the dress. I don't know how this subject came up between you and Seneca, and actually, I didn't care.

I did think Seneca used the situation to put up a wall between us. I was not the kind of person to dress up and put on a dress very often. So if I find something I like, I use it as much as I can. I had shown Seneca a black dress I had bought.

I told her I got black in case I have to use it for the funeral as well. I didn't lie, and at times, I was brutally honest.

For some reason, Seneca told you this information. You were so angry about that. You wanted me to apologize for buying that dress.

I was not going to apologize for buying a dress. I had bought it on the way home from Rochester the day after I was told you were going to die. We didn't even know at that time that you would be getting married.

Just a little reminder, I wore a black dress to Sheena's wedding also. I felt I had done nothing wrong. To me, it just seemed like Seneca wanted to make you angry at me. Why else would she be bringing that up two months later?

About the same time, Seneca came over to the house to confront me about the benefit money. I had been waiting that afternoon for Jen to come over.

I don't recall if anyone else was at the house. She demanded the money and was yelling at me. I reminded her that the money was for the bills. All she had to do was tell me how much she needs, and I would give it to her. But she said your bills were none of my business.

I didn't care about your bill; I cared that you have money to live each month. Trying to take care of things as we had planned was not working. Jen had come over during the argument and had heard everything.

Looking back now, this was such a stupid thing to argue about. I know Seneca loved you. The problem was that she married someone who has cancer and may not be here tomorrow.

None of us asked for this part of life, but we have to deal with it and learn from it.

That is what life should be about, not trying to put one person against another.

The next shocking information I received from you was that you are moving to St. Cloud. I was never sure what was going on to make you come to this decision. You had a trailer house, and it was all paid for.

I know from past issues when you got upset, you refused to talk to me. I guess in your mind, that was my punishment. So I let you vent and tell everyone how awful I was. It didn't matter because when you needed me, you knew your mom would always be there. It didn't matter what you had done. I love you unconditionally forever and always.

Remember that time you didn't have a place to stay. Denny and I let you live in the guesthouse on the farm. You stayed out there and would come in the house and eat with us.

Soon you had a girlfriend out there, and we did not approve of that. Then you had a dog out there, and next thing I knew, the place was trashed even the carpet had burn marks in it.

Denny and I didn't know what to do, so we told you to move out. I think you went a couple of months that time without talking to me, and of course I was the bad mom who had kicked her son out on the curve.

Last week was the county fair. Usually that was the highlight of the summer and the start of fall, a place we went just to run into people we hadn't seen for a while or talked to relatives—something everyone looked forward to. You were still upset with me, so I was not able to bring Bella on any rides or spend any time with her.

One Sunday night, you couldn't breathe. Sheena had gone to your house and even tried to give you a nebulizer treatment. You were finally able to talk after that treatment so it must have helped some.

You were telling me how you could take a breath-in, then exhale, but your chest would not let the next breath-in. I guess you tried all night to get in touch with me.

I came to the hospital on Monday as soon as I got your message. Funny thing, when you were sick, you wanted me to be there.

It didn't matter. You are my son, and there is no place I would rather be.

So your doctor was able to take a liter of fluid off your chest. I think it was easier for you after that.

Your uncle got in trouble for getting in a fight. Someone had called 911, and he ended up going to jail.

He had court today, and Grandpa Leif was waiting for me to go with him.

Grandma was concerned that Grandpa would get so upset he would have a stroke or something.

You had a doctor appointment, and I had promised to go with you. So once again, I was torn between what I should do and what I was asked to do.

My son came first. I had to stay until the doctor had the fluid removed again today.

They were also going to do one more set of X-rays to see how things looked, and after that, you were going home. When I got home that evening, I asked what the doctor said when he was with you. You told me you were sleeping and did not know. Seneca said nothing.

Suddenly you were on your way to St. Cloud again two days after being in the hospital. I guess Seneca had a baby shower. She said she had to attend.

I am sorry you were not able to be home when you weren't feeling good. I can't imagine what that must feel like for you.

You stayed in touch with your sisters pretty much every day. So when you were gone or refused to talk to me, the girls were good to let me know how you were doing.

Sheena said you ended up back in the hospital in St. Cloud on Thursday after you got down there. You had another liter of fluid removed.

My heart ached for you. I don't understand what was going on.

On Saturday, you called to tell me you had been throwing up all day. I asked what was different, and you said Seneca was making you take iron pills. I asked you if she had spoken to the doctor about that; you said no. She just made you take them.

So we talked about how strong the iron can be for your system if your body cannot process it. I told you that when your sister was little, iron would make her throw up or get diarrhea almost like her body was trying to get rid of it.

You were telling me how you had been at a fleet store, and you threw up at the checkout. Then on your way to the bathroom, you did it in front of the next checkout. When you couldn't find the bathroom, you got sick again. You had tried to leave the store, but again, you got sick.

You said you had no warning; it just came out.

I am so sorry. I wanted to just sit down and cry. Why can't you be home at your place instead of down there?

You had pretty much pushed everyone in your life away. You didn't talk to your aunt Tammy, your friend Jen, Uncle Kenny, not even your grandparents, just Sheena and Kayla. I am not sure what you had told Kevin and Karen, but they had not spoken with me in months.

I had been so confused as to why this was going on. So I went to the Internet to read up on information.

One of the interesting things I read said that cancer patients become angry and moody. Once the fluid starts to build up, the brain does not get the oxygen it needs.

I am okay with you being angry but not okay with Seneca pushing to make it worse. Seneca had been pushing a handful of natural vitamins and asking you to change your diet.

I know she really believed this was going to help. But all the doctors told us nothing was going to help at this point. I felt like I was the only person living in reality. You should be eating anything you want and enjoying the time you have left on earth with your daughter.

My mind was thinking about future. You needed to sit down and talk about plans for Bella or making sure you have a will. Even just writing down what you wanted people to have once you are gone. I think I was the only person who thinks about this. Nothing was ever said, the subject was changed, and the answers were never given.

On Monday, you were in the hospital again. Tuesday after you came home, Lori and I went to see you at the house. You were lying on the sofa with your feet up on the coffee table. For the first time, I was shocked and scared at the same time.

Your face was so swollen, I wanted to cry. Lori did cry, but she fought to hold back her tears; she didn't want you to see her breaking down. Your stomach, back, face, and feet were swollen. But you were walking around and sounded good when you talk. Then I looked down at your feet, and I noticed your toenails; they were turning a grey-blue color. I went home that night and cried so hard. I didn't not say a word… I love you, Jerm.

August 20, 2011

Today was August 20. You had made it past your two-month mark and worked on number three.

I had no promises that you would make three months or four. All I know is that each week and day was becoming more and more difficult. It was not only for you but also for me and the rest of the family.

You bought yourself a pocket rocket. I have no idea what made you think this was a good idea. But it was small, and if someone falls off it, they don't have far to go before hitting the ground.

I have to admit it was a cute little bike. I could watch you for hours riding it. No one would know how good it made me feel to see you enjoy yourself like you did when you drove it around the driveway.

On Wednesday night, you came over and wanted to ride on it with Lori. While you were pulling on the cord to start it, you collapsed on the road. I ran outside to help you, but by the time I got there, you were sitting on the side of the road. I was so scared.

Thursday night when I was over to your house. you had been coughing so much because of all the fluid buildup, you passed out for a short time. I was sitting right next to you on the sofa.

Jeremy, I am not ready to see you die. I was so worried at night, and in the morning when you called, you said it had happened again.

On Friday, I took off to work to bring you back to the doctor in Crookston. I was able to talk to your doctor today and let him know what was going on and the changes we had seen. We talked about you passing out and the mood swings and throwing up.

He said all of this was normal. I think once again he had tears in his eyes as he told you to just live every day to the fullest. Have fun when you can. He said he can't heal you, but he would try to make you as comfortable as he can. He asked you to call hospice again.

On the way home, you asked me what I thought. I told you it was up to you. You know hospice works with people who are dying. When you feel you need to contact them, I will be there for you. But no one can push you into anything you don't want to do.

On Friday, you were sick all day when we had gone to Crookston. On Friday night, you wanted to bring your pocket rocket to Auntie Sue's house to show her. Your sister Sheena went with you. You were so sick the entire time there, but it was important for you to go. What can we say? Saturday and you said you were still sick. I am so, so, so sorry. I didn't know what to do.

I went to the house and asked if there was anything I could get for you or do for you. You said nothing. So I talked with you about how I was trying to find someone to give you an airplane ride. You said you were too sick today but maybe on a day when you were feeling better.

We talked about Jen going with you. You said you would go if she went with. Now I would have to talk with her and see what she says.

Funny thing, I put on Facebook that I was looking for someone who would give you a ride. I had an answer from an old-school classmate within hours. I still couldn't get over how every day went by, and we never noticed how people would just drop everything to do something special. Where had my mind been?

I want to tell you how much this last week had meant to me. I had my old Jerm back. It had been so much fun to see you laughing, talking, and sharing with me. I just hope, you know, when the end comes, I will not leave. In fact, a part of me will die with you.

I loved you from the day I knew you were growing inside of me. I will love you till the day God brings us together again.

Each day is but a day to remember, so I will look for the bright side even though my heart is breaking.

I am afraid I am not the strong person you kids think I am. I am slowly being torn down to someone who cannot go a day without tears. I wonder when the tears will dry up, or will they always fall?

The rest of the month of August, we continued doctor visits. The fluid continued to be an issue. Your legs seemed to collect and keep the fluid.

Sad thing was when they removed fluid, it did not take it from your legs or your feet. At times, I looked at you, and I wonder how you walked without any pain. But you didn't complain about that. Most of the problems you actually talked about at this time were the cramps in your legs and the pain in your right shoulder getting worse. When you had the cramps in your legs at times, it caused you to collapse. Seneca had been so good with giving you massages on your legs and feet to help with the cramps.

I know you were hurt, but I think the fear in your eyes overtided the pain you were feeling in your body.

Then I looked at little Bella, and I wondered what she saw and the thoughts that must go through her little mind.

She was losing her daddy. You didn't spend the time playing with her and laughing like you used to.

I know Seneca was there, and she tried so hard to fill in those things with Bella.

Seneca didn't understand that she had not always been there for Bella; you had. I am sure Bella still longs for that relationship with you even if she was only two.

You and Seneca went back down to St. Cloud. I had several text messages from you talking about not feeling well and how you were throwing up so much. Seneca took you to the hospital again in St. Cloud. Once more, they said you were dehydrated.

While you were gone, I continued to work on the airplane ride. You came home from St. Cloud and said you thought you were feeling better and maybe we could do it. So I called and thought the second would be the best.

Of course the pilot was watching for the weather and the wind. I was thinking of you and if you would get sick. We met the pilot Dennis at the Bagley Airport. First time I had ever been there even after living in the area for years.

Jen rode with me. At first, we thought about the three of us going together.

Seneca did not show any interest in the adventure. You tried hard to act like it was no big deal, but I could see something in your eyes that said, "Thank you, Mom." It ended up that you and Jen went along on the ride.

Jen was really good to take the video camera and record this. She also took some good pictures. Dennis even allowed you to take control of the plane at one point. Jen said that your flying scared her. You talked later about how you thought it was so cool to be able to fly.

I looked now at a picture I have. You were looking out the window of the plane. I often wondered what you were thinking in that picture. When you went to heaven, did you see the same thing?

September 7, 2011

You complained about not being able to breathe, so we took you to the ER in Crookston. That time, you stayed overnight because the doctor wanted to remove the fluid in the morning.

That was September 11, and we were on the way to the ER. You were complaining that you couldn't breathe, and the pain in your legs was getting worse. I can't remember what happened that night, but they sent you home.

You had a doctor appointment in Crookston tomorrow. So far this month, we had had three doctor visits and one hospital stay.

So far, the trips to the hospital or the ER had been sporadic. This was however going to increase for us.

The reaction from the staff in the ER during each visit was very important to me and impacted the way I felt about the staff. I had never been a person who runs to the ER for every little cough or cold. But if your child is dying of cancer and you go to the ER, it is because you need help now! I couldn't fix him or make him feel better. Our only hope was that there was something that can be done to make Jeremy more comfortable.

We did not take a forty-five-mile drive to an ER at 10:00 p.m. for an evening drive. At this visit, we were treated like you had just come looking for pain medication.

I remember one of the staff telling me that liver cancer did not go to the heart. I told her the name of your cancer, and her response was that she had never heard of this form of cancer.

I didn't just make this up. It was real, and my son was sick. All I wanted that doctor to do was help making you feel better.

I remember the time you couldn't breathe, and you said you had hurt from your stomach to your shoulder.

The doctor in the ER that night said you had some fluid built up, but they said it wasn't much. So she wanted to give you an enema and send you home.

As soon as the doctor left the room, you grabbed ahold of my shirt and pulled me close to you. You whispered to me. You begged for me to talk to the doctor because you did not want anything going in your butt. I think your words to me that night were "That is an exit only."

I went and told the doctor you did not want to have that done, and you would schedule an appointment with your doctor for the pain.

During the next visit with your doctor, we explained to him how difficult it was when you are not feeling better, and you wanted to go to the ER. I told him how the last time the doctor on call acted like I was making up some name for cancer. He wrote up a sheet we can carry with us, explaining what you have and what medications should be given when you go in. I wish we would have thought of this sooner, but then I didn't know we would make so many trips to the hospitals.

You finally got oxygen delivered to the house on

September 13. This seemed to not only help with the shortness of breath but also seemed to be a sort of comfort for you.

What we didn't know at the time was that you were starting to have panic attacks. You must have had a lot of thoughts going through your mind, which you never talked about.

We had another trip to the ER on September 19. This time, your color had changed, and you were really sick again. Once, the fluid was building up and causing you more discomfort.

They did X-rays and gave you medication for the pain. Two days later, you had a doctor appointment, and you complained about having pains in your legs again.

The trips to the doctor were not always fun. Now think back it amazes me how strong you were.

We used to laugh and joke about sitting in the doctor's office. I remember how you would try to sneak away with a couple extra vomit bags. You always said you never know when you will need one. Bella would get stickers, and you would have two more bags for emergencies. Nothing like making the kids happy.

The next trip back to Crookston you were so sick that day. We were going to drop Bella off with your brother Santos at his apartment so she could play with her cousin Mya.

When we pulled up to the parking lot outside of the building, you opened the car door and started throwing up on the ground.

Santos came running out of the door, and he looked over and saw you throwing up on the sidewalk. He started telling you no to throw up there because people have to walk there like you had any control when this was going to happen.

Santos didn't want to come any closer to the car. You didn't complain; you just said to move the car closer to the parking lot. You asked how much farther we had to go to get to the doctor. I knew you were not feeling well and just wanted the day to end.

When we returned to the apartment complex after the doctor appointment, you were concerned about how far you would have to walk. One flight of stairs, and you couldn't make it any further.

Santos came out of his apartment and wanted to carry you. My boys! Santos wanted to take care of you, and you had your pride. Your determination to not look weak gave you strength to make it up the stairs. We only stayed a short time to visit, picked up Bella, and headed for home. I remember, on the way home that day, you were falling asleep in the car. You woke up quickly with a jump. When I asked you what was wrong, you asked me if your medication made you tired. I told you it did, and then you said, "Good because I was afraid it was the cancer."

I wanted to tell you not to be afraid to fall asleep, but deep down I knew it wouldn't make any difference—some fears a mother cannot take away.

We continued the drive home. I held my hand over yours, holding tight and hoping it would help you sleep.

September 22, 2011

On September 22, we had another trip to the ER. You had been throwing up and were dehydrated again. The doctor had you spend the night in the hospital. I got a kick out of the way you asked if your Bible was packed when you would get ready for another hospital stay.

You told me if you forget to read it, those are the days your pain is worse.

I was noticing that when you get sick and aren't feeling right, you find more comfort in the doctors and hospital. I sometimes wondered if you get more sleep when you are there.

You now joked around about what hospital had the best beds and the special nurses who wait on you hand and foot.

You deserved the attention they were giving you, and it put a smile on your face when you were able to joke or tease with the nurses. This was something you would do till the day you die.

I could see now how teaching you to say thank-you and please as a small child was important, you let everyone know how much you appreciate what they do for you. I was so proud of you.

You got out of the hospital. Seneca insisted on going back down to St. Cloud. I know the two of you are adults who could make your own decisions.

Just letting you know, my thought was that you seemed to be getting sick so often, and you just got out of the hospital. I wish you would just stay home for a couple of days to get your strength built back up.

Once again, you called to tell me about getting sick. You said you had spots on the roof of your mouth. You had a sore throat for the last couple of days.

I had concern because at this time, your body could not handle fighting an infection no matter how small.

We talked about seeing a doctor. You told me you wanted to see your doctor in Crookston and asked me to call and make an appointment for you. When I asked you about a time frame and when you would be home, you just told me to make the appointment. I was able to get you in the following day.

I didn't know at the time that the two of you were looking for apartments in St. Cloud. Yet you were asking me to make an appointment for you because you said that Seneca didn't understand how sick you were. You just said you wanted to come home. When I told you the time, you just said you would be there.

September 27, 2011

You had more fluid removed by your doctor. You had been more days now when you were sick, often throwing up. Funny thing was you and Seneca always seemed to think there was a reason, not the cancer causing you to get sick. Usually, it was because you ate meat or because you ate too soon after taking your medication. This time, it was the trailer house must have mold in it. So you asked to spend the night at our house.

That night, you threw up most of the night. Then you started itching. I was not sure if this was because of your medication or because of your liver not functioning as it should, and the chemicals were building up in your body. Either way, you and I ended up sitting in the living room. I had to scratch your back most of the night. On September 29, you were back to the ER again.

The end of September, you, Seneca, and Bella moved into the basement. I think it gave you comfort to be home. Seneca did not seem to be as comfortable at the house as you were. She stayed in the basement most of the time.

I had to tell you that the weeks I had with you living at home were the most enjoyable times for me. I know you were sick, but when you felt good, it was so much fun.

Once again, we would sit together in the morning, having a cup of coffee and talking. You still sorted through your pills.

Seneca was very good to set up the medications for you, and you trusted her. She had a lot of natural vitamins for you.

Many days, you wouldn't take them as you sorted through you pills you would set them aside and tell me to get rid of them. We always wondered what pill made you nauseous as you would usually run to the bathroom to throw up shortly after taking them.

October 1, 2011

Your fluid was building up again. You still had a cough as well.

We had just finished our morning coffee, and I went into the kitchen. You had been sitting on the sofa but decided to join me in the kitchen. Not far behind you came Bella down the hall running to join us.

Without any notice as you were walking, you fell to the floor, hitting a chair on your way down. We were all concerned about you passing out while you were walking. Bella got so scared and started to cry. It bothered you more that she had seen you fall.

You started to cry. You picked her up to try to comfort her, and she was afraid to be in your arms. No one would ever know the feelings and the tears we had to hold inside that day. Not only for you but also for Bella.

She talked about that fall for a while, but I think she did forget, just like so many other things she would not remember. But I was going to try very hard to make sure she would never forget her daddy and how much you loved her.

It was October 3, and you ended up in the hospital again. This time, you had to stay for a couple of days. Your doctor did not schedule to have the fluid removed from your chest. You were put on antibiotics for the spots in your mouth. He was treating this as if it was strep.

We would be meeting with another doctor to have a drainage tube inserted in your chest. This way, we could remove the fluid at home when it builds up.

The nurses would train Seneca and I on how to do this, so we could treat the discomfort without leaving home.

Once again, I had to let my boss know what was going on and when I would need to take time off work.

Molly, the doctors were supposed to put a drainage tube in Jeremy on Thursday, so I would need to take Thursday and Friday off. They could not put the tube in last week because of an infection Jeremy had.

He did meet with hospice on Friday, but after that meeting, I just don't see how hospice will be an option for him. They told us that with hospice, he would not be seeing a doctor. The nurse would make the decisions for him.

Jeremy found so much comfort in his doctor, so this was not something he wanted. He did agree to have a home health nurse come to the house and help once he got the drainage tube in place.

Having a nurse in the house would hopefully give us some directions. It helped so much to have Jeremy in the house.

I found when I was home, he wanted to be upstairs with me. I noticed this weekend when Kayla was home, he tries to put up such a front when she was around.

He stayed up to watch TV and tried to eat with the family. But when everyone was gone, he told me how sick he felt. Jeremy was really scared to have this tube inserted. My dad had another one of his small seizures or little spells as he called them. Once again, I was torn between running to see how my dad was doing or staying with you.

It was hard for me, and I didn't think anyone really understands.

I hadn't mentioned much about work. I had been working half days since July. I know I could have gone back to work full-time. But I talked with you about it, and you said you wanted me to be available in case you have to go to the doctor.

You needed me, but you refused to put it into those words. Just so you know, Jeremy, I want to be with you ever minute that I can. So even when I was at work for four hours out of the day, I came home to check on you during my break.

I answered my phone when you called, and I was always available if you say you need me.

During your pre-op appointment at the clinic, they said you needed to wait a week for the surgery because of the antibiotics you were taking. Doctor wanted to see if you could wait until next week to have the fluid removed after the surgery. With that way, the fluid had been building up and how much discomfort it caused you. We doubted that it could wait that long. But you were willing to give it a try.

Tonight Lori ran away again. I didn't want to wake you guys up downstairs, so I tried to be very quiet.

I got in the car and went looking for her all over town. I couldn't find her anyplace. I know if I had said anything to you, you would have been up here with me in a heartbeat. I couldn't even begin to count all the times you went looking for her. You always had so much pride in your voice when you would call to tell me you found her. I wonder if Lori would ever know all the times you did that and how you would drop everything to go find her. I would never understand why she did things like this.

I couldn't find her that night. So I just came home and lay down in her bed waiting for her to return.

When she did come home, she was walking so carefully in the living room and the hallway, trying not to make any sound. She didn't even turn on the lights in the bedroom when she came in. Instead, she used some cell phone she had stolen to light her way.

When she saw me lying there, she was shocked. I took the phone from her and said we would talk in the morning. Of course she insisted on a power struggle at that time.

She was telling me she was leaving the house again to return the phone. I told her I would keep the phone, or I could bring it to the police department if she did not know the owner.

I was certain the phone was stolen. She wanted me to call the cops and have her sent away. I just told her that was not what I was going to do. She would be staying home and having consequences for her behaviors.

The next day, I got a call from the school as the parent who owned the phone was there and wanted her phone back. I told the school they had no reason to get involved with the situation, and the mother could call me directly.

The mother did call. She came to the house and picked up the phone. I then found out that Lori has been sneaking out often at nights, and she was not alone. So I contacted the other parents to make them aware of what was happening.

I know Lori was struggling with you being sick, being a teenager, and independent. But really? What happened to kids following house rules?

I ended up sick and on antibiotics by the end of the week as well. I did not want you to catch anything from me, so I was worried. Doctor said I had bronchitis.

You had a doctor appointment, which you ended up missing. You were too sick to drive to Crookston.

Then on October 7, we finally had the get the fluid removed from your chest again. You were not doing well at all. Hopefully now the fluid would build up again prior to surgery.

We now had a health nurse coming to the house to meet with you. Seneca and I had talked with the doctor, and he was able to get a referral for a health nurse to visit maybe once a week.

We thought this would be a good idea since the drainage tube would be put in place, at least until Seneca and I were comfortable with it, and we were sure that you did not get an infection.

We had a birthday for your dad Kevin at the house. Kayla and her boyfriend Matt came home from Grand Forks, and it was so nice to have you kids together.

Santos was the only one missing tonight. You also had made your fourth monthsary. You still were passing out on occasions, but most of the time, you just were not feeling well. Throwing up and being weak we were getting used to, but now you were having more back pain.

October 12, 2011

We were going to get the drainage tube put in. Your dad arrived at the house early in the morning. He was going with us to the hospital.

I drove my vehicle like always. You rode in the front with me. We had to take off around four in the morning. We did fine until we got about thirty-five miles down the road.

I noticed a red light on the dash and asked you why the red light came on. You told me maybe one of the tires was just low, and you said to keep on going.

We then had a tire blowout on the truck. So here we are at four thirty in the morning standing outside the truck on the side of the road.

It was freezing cold and completely dark. I did have a couple of blankets in the back, so your dad (bless his heart) was able to get the spare tire on for us.

Bella was sitting in the back seat in her car seat crying because everyone was outside, and she had to be in the car alone.

I remember how concerned you were about making it to the hospital on time. So you got busy on the phone calling to let them know you had a flat time and would be there as soon as we could. Sometimes I think things like this happened to us, just so God could say, "I am in charge, and things will be done on my time."

The drainage tube was finally inserted. I remember you asking the doctor how long it would be in. He told you a couple of months.

I thought it would never come out. They removed the fluid after the surgery to show Seneca and I what needed to be done. This was the only training we had, so hopefully we got it right.

You had a doctor appointment the next day and ended up in the hospital. This time, your sodium levels were all messed up, and you had a lot of swelling. You stayed in the hospital until October 16. They ended up removing the fluid again on fifteen.

The next three days we had the problems of your swelling increasing throughout your body. Your legs at this time were so swollen that the fluid was draining out through your skin.

At time, your legs would also start to bleed from the pressure of the fluid. When I looked at your legs, I wondered how the fluid could stay there. How could you walk? You must be in so much pain. If there was only some way to relieve it for you, I would.

But our new problem was that your testicles were now swollen. I know if I tried to describe what happened, I just was unbelievable. It was so bad you actually had to carry them when you walked.

When your health nurse arrived, he told us this was common. I asked how we could help you with it. He said there was nothing we could do.

Seneca and I tried very hard to think of some way to make this more comfortable for you. We did try a crazy idea. I took a pair of pantyhose and had you put the top of them over your testicles. We then tied the legs of the pant-yhose around your waist.

This actually helped, believe it or not. I know you tried taking a bath, thinking the water would help, but it didn't. We then tried to drain the fluid from your chest. Nothing seemed to really help. We would just have to wait and pray the swelling would go down on its own.

October 21, 2011

Holly came by to pick up Lori so she could spend the night at her house. Once again, Lori decided to run away.

Only this time, she took Holly's daughter with her. I was not sure who was angrier, but if I was a betting person, I was sure Holly was in the lead.

I was used to Lori pulling her little stunts, and they didn't affect me like they did other people. Besides, my son had cancer. What could be worse than that?

Lori ran, but she came back and faced the consequences. I had no place to run to, and neither do you. We will fight to the end.

We were now draining your fluids at home, usually about every three days. You still got shots in your stomach twice a day.

Medications seemed to stay the same. Most days, you lay in the guest bedroom upstairs so you were close by.

Seneca and I were now very familiar with our new routine—cleaning the tube you had in your chest and cleaning the one we hooked on you.

The bag of the fluid drained into was vacuum-packed, so it just sucked the fluid out. Once we got the tubes cleansed everything in place, you usually would keep us informed on how fast it should drain. If you felt any pain, we usually would stop.

I was surprised to find out that the nurse who came to the house had no idea how to do this. My friend Linda who had just finished up with her nursing degree said she had never been trained on how to do this either.

October 22, 2011

October 22 was Grandpa Leif's birthday. You had been sick all day, so you didn't want to go anyplace. I went over to their place long enough to tell my dad I loved him and wished him a happy birthday.

He was concerned about you. He said he prayed for you every time you come to his mind.

My dad kept telling me he was praying that God would heal you. I watched as you were sick, and I just didn't know. I did know that God gave me a beautiful son, and at some time, I was going to have to give you back to him.

So for the next few days, we drained the fluid from your chest whenever you told us you were getting uncomfortable.

We made your doctor appointments. We ended up with ER run on the twenty-four and doctor on the twenty-seven.

Your muscles were cramping up more often. The muscle relaxers and medications just didn't seem to help. You were now starting to increase the amount of morphine you take.

On October 30, Seneca and Bella left for St. Cloud again. You chose to stay home with me because your feet were so swollen, and you said your ankles hurt.

I removed the fluid from your chest that evening. I was starting to get frustrated and didn't understand how Seneca could just get up and leave you. I couldn't leave you at all, and when I was not with you, I worried about you and wanted to just run home to be with you.

Happy Halloween!

You and I stayed home to hand out candy. I thought it was cute how you tried to save the *good stuff* for your nieces and your nephew.

You waited for them to get to the house. When people stopped by the house, you would open the door and hand out the candy. Several people asked you how you were feeling, and you always told them you were doing great. You were going to beat this cancer.

By that evening, you became really sick again. You had diarrhea and throwing up all day.

There was nothing I could do to help you. So once again, you ended up in the ER.

You had another hospital stay in Fosston this time. You were dehydrated again, and your sodium levels were low. When you got out of the hospital, the health nurse would be making a visit to the house.

November 2, 2011

I removed fluid again from your lungs, and the health nurse was here for a visit. Your blood pressure was low today, but he said that could be due to your medications.

You were feeling better later in the evening and went to Bemidji with Grandpa and Grandma. You decided to spend the night with your dad and Karen.

This time, I got a phone call saying you had been sick, and it was hard for someone to take care of you when they were not use to it. I was told you really needed to be at home so I can take care of you.

But changing your mind and keeping you from going someplace when you want to go was not easy. You were kind of stubborn. The nurse had told you not to drive, but when someone told you not to do something, you wanted to do it.

I know you stayed at your dad's house that night because you were not feeling good and didn't want to drive home. But I think it was good for you to spend time with your dad, so I was not going to stop you. He was so close, and yet each day went by.

On November 3, we had another doctor appointment. I think Seneca had plans to meet us at the clinic. She would be coming straight from St. Cloud.

The doctor seemed concerned about the fluid buildup in your legs and feet today. He talked about changing one of your fluid pills.

We also talked about how your hands were starting to get shaky. At times, it was very difficult for you to hold on to things like a cup of coffee. He said not to worry about it because it did go away and was not happening all the time.

You talked with me again today about being afraid to fall asleep. If only I could hold you in my arms when you sleep and let you know that I was not going to leave you. I wonder if then you would be able to sleep better.

When I remember back to when you were a baby, you used to fall asleep so easily. Sometimes you would fall asleep when you were eating in the high chair. When you went to sleep in your car seat, you wouldn't even wake up when we would bring you in the house and change your clothes. Now it was something that scared you. I am so sorry; I cannot scare this monster away.

For those who have cancer, I am sure the fears and the unknown is more than you wish to even talk about. I only know as a parent watching and caring for my son what it is like for me.

People don't make fun of you or see this as a weakness. You don't know how to deal with it and try to just pretend it isn't happening.

You would even get upset with me if I tried to talk to the doctor myself for answers. I remember how you always asked if you looked sick. I never thought you did.

We didn't see the changes that took place with your body or how you looked to other people. The times I thought the color of your skin would look dark, or your eyes seemed to look so tired. I never said anything. The obvious change was always the swelling.

That evening, you had more muscle pain in your back, legs, and arms. Seneca tried to massage your muscles, but it just didn't help. You held on to a blank, and I could see your fists tighten around the blanket as the pain increased. Words were just not enough. We took you back to the hospital for a pain shot, and you ended up spending the night again.

You came home on October 4 around three in the afternoon. You were very sleepy that day, and when you did wake up, all you could talk about was going hunting the next morning.

Lori was going to get up and go with you, but you didn't go. You went into the hospital again that night for another pain shot and didn't get home until 11:30 p.m.

On Saturday, you got up early to go hunting as you had planned. Lori went with you today. It was funny how you could bring out the best of her. She enjoyed spending as much time with you as she could. So even though she had to get up early, she didn't complain and was ready to go with you.

Lori talked about you falling asleep, and she was told to watch for the deer. When she saw one, you got up and tried to take a shot, but you missed.

You didn't complain at all during the day, but by evening, you were in pain again. You went to the hospital to see if you could get a shot for the pain.

We had been invited to your sister Sheena's house to celebrate Damian, Zoey, and Fred's birthdays. Sheena decided to combine the three birthdays' since they were all so close. I even got a picture of you and your dad wearing those goofy birthday hats. Now years later, the picture had disappeared, and all I have was a memory of the event, and I tried to imagine the hat on your head.

Seneca had left for St. Cloud again today, so it was just you and me again tonight, kiddo.

November 6, 2011

You were determined to go hunting again. You got up early, and I got up with you to help make some coffee and pack up some snacks for your day.

I took a picture of you standing in the laundry room with your gun and all dressed in orange. I worried about you so much because I didn't want you to be alone.

Lori went with you for a couple of hours this morning. Then you came home and dropped her off. You got your medications and headed out again in the afternoon with your dad.

You called me and were so excited because you got a little doe. The story you told when you got home was that you shot the deer. Both you and your dad started to run out in the field. You said you forgot that you couldn't run, and you collapsed in the field.

Your dad took you home that night. Your cousin Jesse helped you bleed the deer, and you hung it in your uncle Mike's garage until we can get it cut up.

Writing this all down is so difficult. I feel as if I am reliving each nightmarish day over again.

I miss you so much. I can see in my mind you were falling and not being able to get up.

I wish I could have helped you. I should have been there more.

I could still see the times of joy and excitement, how your eyes would seem to sparkle. But in the last few months, I could see the pain and fear in your eyes. I had to stand to the side and watch as the cancer ate away at your body. Seneca and I could see as you became so sick and weak more often. You wouldn't let anyone know what was really going on. You tried so hard to be strong, and up to the very end of your life, you were strong. You went from being my little boy to becoming my hero. Right in front of my eyes, you changed, and you didn't even know it.

I remember when you lost your uncle Steve to cancer at the beginning of the year. You told me then that you wished you could take it away from him.

Later after you became sick, you said, "Never make a wish you don't intend to keep." You couldn't take it away from someone else, and cancer is not something anyone wishes for.

If words held that much power, I would wish for you to be well. I know I couldn't change anything. I did, however, pray that if God had it in his plans to heal you, I would like him to do it quickly so you no longer have to suffer. All we could do was to pray for strength as we fought this battle together. You were never alone, my son.

November 7, 2011

This morning by one, you started to get sick. It all started with you running to the bathroom to throw up, then you had diarrhea on top of that.

I had never seen you this sick. By 4:00 a.m., you were asking me to call the ambulance to come and get you. We only lived about seven blocks from the hospital, and I knew it would be quicker just to drive you there.

I started up the car and got you there as fast as I could. My heart was just breaking. I was so upset when we got to the hospital, we had to wait until five thirty before a doctor even arrived.

You had been throwing up in the hospital and running to the bathroom. You were in a wheelchair because you didn't even have the strength to hold yourself up.

At one time, you even messed your pants, so they had to put a diaper on you. You were so sick you didn't even care. When the doctor did arrive, the first thing she said was "We need to come up with a better plan for Jeremy and how to handle him when he is sick."

I was so hurt. This was my son she was talking about.

You were sitting right there and so sick. I told her how you had been feeling all night, and I was afraid you were dehydrated as well.

You were dehydrated, and your blood cells were elevated; sodium levels were low.

You ended up getting a room at the hospital again. They were going to let you out that evening, but you ended up spending the night.

So for the last thirty-nine hours, I had only gotten two hours of sleep. But I enjoyed just sitting with you and talking with you when you were awake. Watching you sleep, I found myself watching every breath you took.

At one point when you were sleeping, it seemed as if you were not breathing. I didn't see your chest moving. It seemed like it had been a long time without a breath. I thought you were gone. I was going to call the nurse.

Then I thought, *No, I want you to be able to just fall asleep and not have to struggle for your last breath.*

As I was looking down at you, you opened your beautiful blue eyes and looked at me. I held your hand till you feel back to sleep.

I didn't want you in any pain, and right now, this was where we need to be. You never knew what had happened or the thoughts that had gone through my mind. I wonder if in the Bible, this was what Mary meant by pondering things in her heart about Jesus.

The next day, we got out of the hospital around 11:00 a.m. We went to A&W to have lunch with your uncle Wade, your cousin Adam, Grandma DeeDee, and Grandpa Leif. We had to be back at the house to meet with your health nurse at 1:00 p.m., and my boss was going to be at the house to meet me at 1:30 p.m.

We had a crazy day planned. I knew when we got home, I had to get the fluid drained from your lungs, so even though your nurse was there, we went to the bedroom to get it done.

My boss arrived, and she had brought supper over for the family. This was a blessing since we now had a bunch of people to feed.

She informed me that my family medical leave was all used up. I had no sick leave or vacation time remaining. Coworkers could no longer donate time for me to miss work.

I had no idea how long I would go without a pay-check. She said that she had to go before the county board to see if they will hold my job for me. My only thought at the time was it was okay.

God would provide for us and make sure that we were able to make it through this.

I had more important things to worry about. Truth is I didn't even feel like my job was something I could take before God in prayer. You were all that mattered to me. My time with you was counting down. I didn't know it then, but I only had a month left with you. I wanted to make memories every day and be close to you.

I wonder what other people do to cover the expenses of living day-to-day when you were going through something like this.

We had Denny's paycheck and credit cards. I wonder how many years it would be before I was no longer paying for this time with you.

I had forgotten to mention that Kayla's boyfriend Matt was also staying at the house. He had decided to stay here and go hunting with you as well this year.

November 9, 2011

The afternoon of November 9, you and Matt went out hunting together. You didn't see anything today. But I guess you made it pretty clear to Matt that you could get more deer, and you intended to go out no matter what.

Matt acted like he just wants to get one deer. I know he would like it to be a big buck.

Your legs were so swollen, and they were bleeding more. I couldn't believe how strong you were and how you could keep going. Your legs looked like they would hurt just to try to stand on them and let alone to try walk.

While you and Matt were out hunting, you called me. You said you had fallen asleep and had accidentally wet your pants. You felt so bad, and you were crying.

Matt, being a nurse, didn't say anything. He felt bad for you, but there was nothing we could do. Let's put it aside and press forward.

By midnight, you were having really bad muscle cramps again. Seneca tried her best to sit with you and massage your legs, but you just didn't seem to get comfortable.

At the next doctor appointment, the doctor said the inferior vena cava was totally blocked. There was no way to help with any of the fluid in your legs.

We talked about pain management today. He said you were on the strongest fluid pills, and your morphine was every four to six hours, plus you had a pain patch along with muscle relaxer. He said we could increase some of the meds to three to four times a day.

The doctor said you would be very sleepy with the increase in medications, but this didn't seem to bother you. We were all just hoping this would help with some of the cramps you had in your muscles, and that we won't have to make ER visits so often.

November 11—another day of hunting. This time, it was Denny, Matt, and you.

I know you guys had not been gone very long that morning before I got a phone call.

This time, it was Denny. He was calling to tell me he had gotten his deer. No one shot it. Denny said he hit it with his pickup. He didn't see any damage, and the pickup was still working. No one got hurt.

The next day, your nurse was here again. You were in pain during most of the visit with him. We ended up making another trip to the ER that evening. You sure didn't like when anyone, especially the nurse, talked with you about driving. It seems to me the subject should be brought up once to the caregiver and then let them remind you of the safety concerns. The subject only seemed to make you angrier.

Kayla came home. Uncle Kenny and Aunt Kelly were here this weekend. So the house was full. You had been working so hard to get up and go hunting.

You went out again with Matt on November 12. The increase in your pain patch seemed to be helping.

You tried to go to church with Sheena on Sunday but had a difficult time staying awake. You went to the bathroom often, and at times, you still wet your pants when you were sleeping. You were so worried because you had been seeing blood in the toilet after you went to the bathroom.

The health nurse checked it out and thought it was just because you were on so many pain medications; you were getting constipated.

On November 14, you had your first really difficult panic attack. Seneca and I went to drain your fluid from your lungs today, and halfway through, you asked us to stop because it was causing you pain. We stopped, and then you said you were having a difficult time breathing.

You said it felt like your throat was closing up on you. We tried to give you oxygen, but you said it wasn't helping. We finally got you to laid down and rest for a while.

When you woke up, you wanted to go to Bemidji with Seneca. Sometimes you just wanted to get out of the house even more so as your anxiety levels increased.

The next day, we started with you throwing up again. I was not sure what was going on with you. You told me something just didn't feel right. This lasted all day.

That night, you were in the bathroom lying on the floor. I sat down next to you, and you laid down in my lap. You asked me about dying. I felt like we were going through the whole experience of Mayo Clinic again, just you and me sitting on the bathroom floor.

You wanted answers, and I didn't know what to say. I told you tonight that the fight was a hard one, and I think the cancer was winning.

We sat there on the floor and cried. Why did you ask me? I didn't want to be the one to say these words. I didn't want to hurt you with words you didn't want to hear.

Seneca got mad at me because of the conversation we had. I am sorry, but I think you wanted to hear the truth. You were not getting any better. Lately you had been sick all the time. When you were sick, you get scared, and sometimes new symptoms showed up.

I felt lost like I didn't know what to do. Who was there to help me? Hopefully we could talk again soon.

After we talked, you were crying and called your dad. He came over, and I will never forget how you ran to him, reaching out your arms.

When you were hugging him and crying, you kept telling him that you were dying. I remember how he looked past you like he didn't know what to say. All that went through my head was Kevin to hug him and give him the support he needed. I guess a dad doesn't know what to do either.

Seneca called me at work today, said you were threatening to call the cops on her. When I got home, you told me that you wanted her out of the house. You wanted to go to the doctor, and she wouldn't let you go. You were upset because you said she didn't understand what you were going through. I tried to explain that if we went to the ER today, we would be late for the appointment in Grand Forks.

This appointment you had scheduled was at the cancer center; you didn't care. You just wanted to go to the hospital. We were able to calm you down long enough to take a short nap. You finally fell asleep sitting at the kitchen table. Your dad arrived, and we went to the appointment together.

The doctor sat down and tried to work on a plan for your medications. She stopped the pain patches and increased your morphine.

She also stopped the oxycodone and the muscle relaxer you were taking. The morphine was increased to 100 mg three times a day. We were supposed to return for a follow-up visit in two weeks.

The changes in your medication seemed to be helping. You seemed to be a little sleepier, and the anxiety wasn't as bad as it was.

The pain seemed to be more managed as well. Your nurse was back at the house again, and he said you would not qualify for hospice because you go to the hospital when you were not feeling good.

He said hospice plan was for the patient to stay home and not have the doctors involved. I tried to explain to him how you felt the comfort of knowing someone was there to care for you.

I know how much you depend on Seneca and I being there for you, but when you got scared, we just didn't do the job well enough.

The nurse also talked about how your cancer was progressing and how things were just going to get worse.

I was just thinking to myself at this time. How could things get worse? I was so drained the way it is now.

You were right, Jeremy. We don't understand how you felt or what you were going through.

Your uncle Obie called and said he had gotten a big buck today. You called him back when you woke up. You started to cry on the phone because you had not been there with him. I felt so bad this in not something you would have done in the past.

I am sure Obie had no idea how to respond to your call. No one ever said that a person would go through these mood changes and personality changes.

You told your nurse that you didn't think anything had changed. I tried to remind you how the medications had changed and seemed to be helping.

Seneca and I drained more fluid but only had a little built up today.

November 18, 2011

I sent a note out to my coworkers to let them know how things are going.

First off, I wanted everyone to know it was so difficult to accept help from anyone. I was learning that it was a blessing. Meals seemed to appear on days when things were so crazy for our family. I don't know maybe life is crazy all the time. I have lost track.

Since Jeremy moved into the house, it had been easier to me his needs and be available for him. After he had the drainage tube put in, his wife and I drained the fluid off his chest every three days.

The last week, this had been causing him more pain. So he would usually stop the procedure before we were done. The swelling in his feet and legs had been pretty bad over the last six weeks. The doctors had said this was because of the clogged vein that brought the fluid back up from the legs and lower body back to the liver.

He was on the strongest diuretic they could put him on, so there was nothing else they could really do for that. Good news! We were getting used to the fat feet and toes. He had also started having some jerking in his arms that he couldn't control. This was also because of the liver.

So at times, he had a hard time holding on to thing.

This was difficult for him. He didn't like when people see him shake or drop things. We did have nursing service coming to the house twice a week.

Seneca and I wanted to have hospice, but we had a few issues with that.

One of the medications he took to control the blood clots was considered a treatment and very costly. Hospice will not work with clients who are still receiving treatment.

The other issue was that over the last ten days, Jeremy had been going through a complete personality change.

OCD and anxiety are not fun to live with. So when something new happened, he felt like the only way to deal with this was to call the hospital.

Sometimes he called three times a day. This was something we couldn't control, and if we didn't let him, he got angry.

The good news was that Jeremy was able to go hunting this year. He got a deer the second day out.

Of course Denny still must cut it up, but Jeremy was excited. He liked to share his hunting story with anyone who would listen, including doctors and nurses.

His little girl didn't understand what was going on. I pray that she will not remember what she sees.

I wanted to say thank you to everyone for all that you do. You will never know how each of you have touched my heart.

November 19, 2011

On the nineteen, you went hunting again today. You went out with your cousin's husband. I didn't know it at the time, but I talked with him later, and he shared the story with me. He said how you had been all excited about hunting that day, but you had fallen asleep in the pickup.

He said he went to wake you up when he saw a deer running. When you woke up, you noticed that your pants were wet. You were so embarrassed, and you questioned him why he didn't laugh at you. He said he never would have laughed. So you tried to stand in front of the heater to dry off your shorts.

During that time, another deer came running out. You told him you couldn't shoot because your pants were down. I didn't have that wonderful memory of that day, only what I had been told. My memory of the day was very different. For me, the day was the start of a long road to the end.

Seneca took off for St. Cloud again with Bella. You had been gone in the morning and called to let me know you had gotten a deer.

Later in the afternoon, you called to tell me that you were sick and had been throwing up. I asked you if you wanted a ride home and said I would come to get you. You told me you were at your aunt's house and that you had a ride home.

You just didn't feel very good. That night, you spent the night at your dad's house. His wife Karen called me that night and told me how sick you were. She said she didn't think you should be going any place.

She also said she had talked with Seneca and asked her why she had left her husband when he was so sick. She said she asked Seneca why she even married you when she knew this was what she was going to have to face. Seneca told her on the phone that it was because she worried about Bella.

The next morning, you got up early and went hunting again. Plans were that you would be leaving with your cousin and riding to St. Cloud with her to meet up with Seneca. But by two that afternoon, you called me and said you were too sick to make the trip. All you wanted to do was come home.

I called your dad and Karen, but they were in Bemidji watching a movie and couldn't bring you home.

I was not sure what was going on, but you called me several times to tell me how sick you were.

You wanted to come home by six thirty that night your aunt brought you home. I don't remember what was going on that day for me or why I was unable to come and get you. But looking back, I wish I had picked you up. I would have had another half hour of time with you.

You complained of having a lot of pain when you got home and had been running to the bathroom frequently.

That night, you started to see a little black dog. You were walking into the bedroom and asked who's dog it was. I thought you were joking because I didn't see a dog. You said he had been following you, and you were okay if the dog wanted to sleep in your bed.

You said that the dog had also been following our dog Shaggy. You asked what the dog's name was, and I didn't know what to tell you.

So I thought about a black dog I couldn't see. I told you his name was Shadow. You were so weak that night you fell just walking into the living room.

Denny and I both had to lift you up. Seneca was called, and she came home. You told us tonight that you thought you were going to die before morning.

That night, your breathing changed when you were sleeping. Seneca came to wake me up, and we both just laid on the bed with you.

We were quietly talking about how much we loved you. We thought this was the end, and then out of nowhere, you asked us what we were talking about.

You said, "I can hear you."

I got up and went to my bed feeling like I had just been caught doing something wrong.

Seneca and I never did tell you what we were talking about.

The next morning as we sat in the living room, you looked at me for a long time without saying a word. Then you told me, "Mom, I think it is time I turn in my two-week notice."

I asked what you mean by that.

You picked up your coffee and took a sip. Your words rang in my ears as you told me, "We both know I won't be here to spend Christmas with you."

I know you were not getting any better, but my mind couldn't even think of what Christmas or any other day would be like without you in it.

At the next visit with your doctor, he said the symptoms you were going through were normal. Only most people are already lying in a bed dying. He said you have so much courage and strength, not to mention the fight to hang on to every bit of your life.

He said your feet were already starting to model. All I could think was that I was not ready for this. I didn't want you to die.

When we got home that day, I called my boss. I remember being on my knees of the side of the bed, my phone in my hands as the tears just kept falling. I cried out to her, "Molly,

I just can't do this anymore. I can't go back to work because I know I don't have much time left with Jeremy."

I don't remember the words she said to me, but I remember her tone. She always spoke to me with understanding and concern. I didn't need to worry about work; I needed to be with my son.

My friend Holly had just lost her dad to cancer. We had been talking often about how we were both stuck in this nightmare, and we knew when everything was over, our lives would never be the same.

Her dad passed away, and now I was getting closer to losing you. I had no way to turn back the time, and I had to walk through this battle with you.

My heart was hurting more every day, and all I could think about was staying strong for everyone else. Dear God, please give me the strength I need.

We picked up birthday cards for Bella today. I wanted you to just sign them, so as the years go by in the future, she would still receive cards from her daddy.

The cards were there. I don't know if you will ever write on them.

You did call Jen tonight and asked her to come over for a movie night. I don't think you watched a movie.

You guys took turns rubbing each other's feet. I got the video camera out so I could capture the memory.

When it came time for Jen to leave, you took her aside and talked with her about dying. You told her that you knew she was dying, and that life wasn't supposed to be like this. But whoever go to heaven first would have to wait for the other person.

After I asked you how you knew that Jen was dying, all you said was "Mom, I know things."

I love how you took every moment to tell me you loved me. When I stood in the kitchen, you came up behind me just to rub my back and show your love. I am so going to miss those little things you do.

You called pastor and asked him to come over. So he was here. He had prayer and communion with you today. I had never been so proud of you as I was today. You prayed from your heart, and it was such a blessing to listen to.

You talked about how important forgiveness is, and that people should not have any anger. You didn't want anyone to ever feel angry that you had cancer. I remember just looking at you and thinking, *Wow, that's my son!*

November 22, 2011

We had so much company the next couple of days. I couldn't even name them all. But the wonderful thing is that you even took time to pray with y our uncle Obie and aunt Janie. You fought so hard today to stay up and spend time with each person.

Your nurse was here as well. Then Kayla came home. I don't mention it much, but Sheena was so good to stop by and check on you. The two of you had always had a close relationship. I think she missed you not being next door to her right now.

She always said it was so nice to just yell out the window to you, and you would answer her right away.

Your sisters were going to have a huge adjustment to make when they no longer have their brother.

November 23, 2011

You were sleeping more today than you had in a long time. You were getting up to go to the bathroom.

Seneca and I drained your fluid again. My friends Linda and Wendie were here today. I told them how you didn't think you would be here for Christmas this year. Linda thought we should put the Christmas tree up, so we had the tree up with lights and everything. Linda had Bella outside playing on the swing set for a while.

It was such a beautiful day. You just wouldn't believe it was the end of November, and it feels like September.

Uncle Kenny and Kelly, along with their boys, arrived in the evening. Tomorrow was Thanksgiving, and I had so much to do.

Really, I didn't feel like doing anything. I didn't want it to be the last Thanksgiving with you, and I didn't know if you would be here for Christmas. So if I close my eyes and just pretend, maybe tomorrow will never come.

Happy Thanksgiving!

All five of my kids were home today. Yes, we took pictures, we laughed, and we really enjoyed just being together. This was the day I took that picture of you and Santos both sitting in chairs with your hands behind your heads—so different yet alike.

I didn't think you were feeling very good and had a hard time just standing up. You were sleepy but tried so hard to stay awake and visit with everyone.

I think you sat in the kitchen by the food just so you could do something to keep your eyes open.

Your dad and Karen came over here for dinner as well. That afternoon, Grandpa Leif, Grandma DeeDee, Aunt Tammy, Uncle Mike and Aunt Janet, along with Kenny and Kelly were all here. My only sibling missing was Tony. It was a busy day and a full house. You insisted on staying up and visiting with everyone. We took lots of videos and enjoyed the day.

The most memorable about Thanksgiving this year was that I forgot to buy black olives, so you and Kayla went all over town trying to buy some. You finally ended up going to the deli and buying a container of cut up olives. I don't think I will ever forget them again.

I don't know who thought it was a big mistake if it was you or Kayla. I do know that every family get-together after that day, Kayla had reminded me to get the olives. Funny how one little thing becomes a tradition I am now reminded all the time to get the olives.

November 26, 2011

The twenty-six was a difficult day—one I still remember years later.

Seneca was making plans on leaving for St. Cloud. I don't mind if she goes, but I didn't think you were healthy enough to travel any distance.

You told Seneca that you wanted to go. But you told me you were not feeling well and didn't want to.

I remember saying that I was afraid you could even fall asleep in the car and die. What kind of memory would that be for Bella? But you finally decided that the two of you would go, but Bella would stay home with me.

Just as you and Seneca were getting ready to leave, you went to the door and made it onto the deck. You started to throw up. You put your arms around your wife, and you begged her to stay home with you. But she still chose to leave with Bella.

My heart again was just breaking for you. I knew you didn't feel good, and you wanted her here with you.

You threw up many times that day. After this, you got sleepy, and the rest of the day you just wanted to lay down.

You didn't eat much at all today. You said several times that you were hungry, but then you never had the energy to eat.

Your blood pressure was low today at 82/64, and your pulse was at 100.

November 27, 2011

Seneca and Bella came home today. We removed a full bottle of fluid from your lungs today.

Your aunt Tammy was here. I had told her how you had been too tired to even eat. So she came out and made some cereal for you and sat by your bed to feed you. You ate everything for her. But the rest of the day, you were very sleepy.

At times, you didn't even respond when we tried to talk to you. Your breathing changed today as well. At times, it was very heavy, other times shallow. Sometimes you stopped all together.

It had been hard for you when company came. You seemed to get very anxious and tried to stay awake.

Today was the first day that you didn't respond to anyone. Tammy sat with you most of the day.

The next day, your anxiety was way up there again. You kept insisting on going to the hospital. But you didn't know why you wanted to go. You would walk over to the window and just look outside.

One time, I asked what you were doing, and you told me you were just breathing. Kayla came home, and I think that helped some with the wanting to leave. You were able to sit down and stay home with her.

November 29, 2011

On the twenty-nine, we went through another day of extreme anxiety. We were unable to even get you to sit down and rest. You took your medications, but you refused to sleep.

Adding on confusion today to your anxiety just made things worse. At one point, you forgot who Bella was. When you realized what had just happened, you started to cry because you couldn't understand how a father could forget his little girl.

Your nurse was over. He said that we only had a couple of days, maybe a week left.

Pastor stopped by, and you had a good talk with him. You talked about riding on the school bus with him and how you would handle the kids.

It was so cute. You told him if the kids got too loud, you would turn around and say, "God bless you." I will never forget that conversation.

I also talked with the pastor about a funeral service.

Your grandparents and your aunt Tammy were here today along with your dad. Your cousin Jesse stopped over this evening while he was on duty. It was his coffee break. You so wanted to sit with Jesse and visit with him. You wanted to have coffee with him, so you filled up your big cup. You were so shaky. I knew you were going to spill it. But you kept telling me you were fine you wouldn't spill.

I know you wanted Jesse to see you as being just fine and normal. You never liked it when other people were around, and Seneca or I offered to help you.

After you left the room, I had the chance to talk with Jesse. He said that if you would die at home, there were things we have to take care of first. If we don't, your death would be considered unattended because you are not on the hospice list, so they would end up sending your body to the cities for an autopsy.

We didn't want that to happen, so we had work we need to do. We had to have a doctor sign a death certificate. Seneca took care of that with your doctor in Crookston.

We also needed to let the funeral home know so that they would just come and pick you up.

It was going to be difficult to think about these things now, and we had no idea when the end was coming. I know this was a bad dream, and I needed to wake up. I did not want to do this.

Bella's mom called tonight. I had been sitting in the kitchen with your aunt Janie, my friend Wendie, and Kayla.

She wanted to find out if you were dying. She said she had been told that you only have thirty-six hours to live.

I told her you had not been given a time since we had been in the Mayo Clinic, and that was five months ago.

She said she was just concerned about you.

I brought up the subject of seeing Bella, and I told her that if she wanted to come and spend time with Bella, all she had to do was call.

I would make sure that she and Bella could spend time together. I didn't know it then, but those witnesses to that conversation would soon become important for me. I know now that she was just working on her own plans of when she was going to be able to take Bella.

I was still having bad nightmares. I had had some that just didn't get out of my head.

I cried all day after I would have one of those dreams. The last one I had was when you and I were talking, and you told me you just wanted to get away from everything. I told you I would take you wherever you wanted to go.

We went to the airport and got into an airplane. While we waited for the plane to take off, you were leaning against the window, and you said, "Mom, I don't feel good. I think I just want to go home."

I remember walking with you leaning on me, trying to get you home.

All I wanted to do was to take care of you. Sometimes the nightmare I lived with during the day became just as real at night. How do I get over this?

CHAPTER 3

Saying Goodbye, End of Life Care

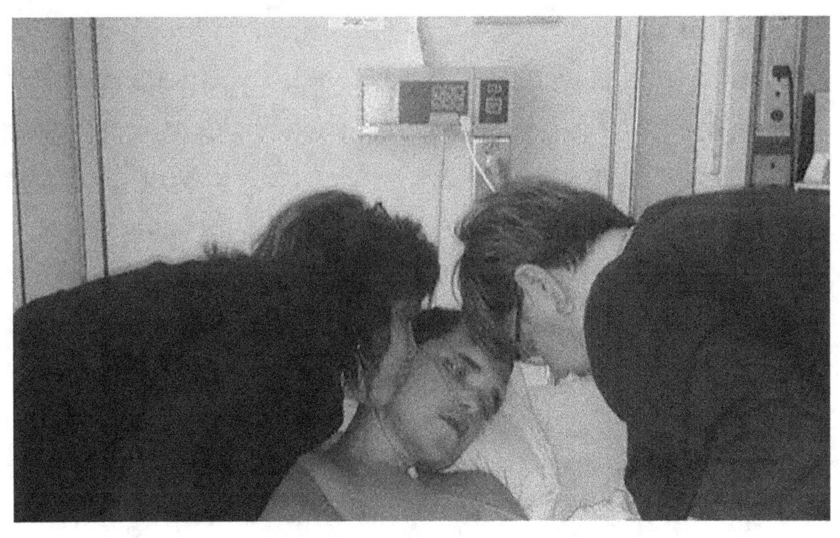

November 30, 2011

November 30 was the last day you were at home. It was such a painful day to remember.

Your aunt Tammy came over to the house. She was going to stay there with you because Seneca and I had things we had to do.

We went to the funeral home in the morning to talk with them. I explained the situation that you had cancer, and we did not know how long you had left to live.

We did not want you to get sent down to the cities and wanted to know what they needed from us for things to go smoothly.

After that meeting, they said all we needed to do was to call them when the time came.

I am so sorry, Jeremy. I don't want to make that phone call *ever*. My heart hurt for every mom whoever has to go through this.

Tammy had stayed at the house with you when we had been at the funeral home. I think she sent us three to four messages in the hour we were gone. She said you had been extremely anxious and were waiting for us to come home. I don't remember a time that we had both left together.

You did not like having both of us gone away from the house.

Of course your morning had started out bad as you had been downstairs with Bella and when you were coming up the steps you had fallen down. Any time something like that happened it scared you.

When Seneca and I got back to the house, you walked outside because you wanted to go for a ride. I looked out the window, and you were lying on the ground outside. You had fallen again.

Your anxiety was the worse I had seen up to now. You couldn't calm down; you didn't want to eat, sleep, or sit down at all. The only thing on your mind was to get out of the house.

We decided to take a ride to one of the nearby lakes. I thought maybe just sitting down by a calm lake would help, just being outside with nature and trees. But we needed to pick up some snacks because I didn't know how long we would be gone.

We went to the grocery store to pick up our supplies for the little road trip. Walking up the aisle at the store just looking at the items we were hungry for, you suddenly said, "Can we just go to the grocery store and get it?"

Yeah, we were at the store. Then when we were getting ready to leave, and Tammy had to go to the bathroom. You told her not to use the one at the store. You insisted that we go to the gas station. You said you wanted her to have a clean bathroom.

We then went to the lake. We just sat there and thought. I am not sure what was going on in anyone's thoughts, but I never thought this would be the last tie for us to sit by a lake together.

I know that trip was important to you because you were calm and seemed to just enjoy being outside. I was so glad that the weather was still warm and comfortable.

Once we returned home, the anxiety returned. We called the health nurse and asked him to come over.

He brought with him the hospital social worker. We sat down to meet with them concerning your care. They talked about putting you in the hospital here but said the hospital was under construction, and they were not sure if there was a room for you.

Seneca and I told them that you had not been on the shots for your blood clots since Sunday. We had decided to stop these shots because we could see you were going downhill healthwise. We just didn't think it made sense to cause you any more discomfort, and we knew it was not doing you any good at this time.

After we talked about the options we had and talking to your doctor, the decision was to put you on Haldol to help with the anxiety. So your nurse went up to the drugstore to pick up the prescription. They were going to give you a shot tonight, and then we were to take you to the hospital in Crookston.

Your doctor was going to put you in the hospital for end-of-life care. This time, we are told you could die tonight, tomorrow, or maybe a couple of days. No one knows what the next few hours or days will hold for us.

How many times could your heart be crushed, and you still stood up to take more? I don't think you understood what was going on at that time. I know we tried to include you in the conversations, but I really think you thought we were just going to the hospital.

Like I said, you had been a part of every conversation we had. It had been your choice to go to the hospital at that time.

I am not sure if you know then that you would not be home again. I was surprised when you turned to hug your health nurse, and you thanked him for being there for you over the last couple of months.

One of my friends had stopped over with some food, and you hugged her and thanked her for the food. She had brought over a box of items that we could just grab and go. It was so nice to have that because the next week, we would be doing just that.

After you had your shot, it seemed to help right away. You were able to sit down in the living room and just rest. I had taken my last picture of you in the house that night sitting on the sofa with Lori, and I think Kayla was there.

I don't really know that picture was saved on my phone, and when the phone died, so did many of my pictures. I never did get to have it saved or made into a photo.

On the way to the hospital, we stopped at the gas station just to pick up some pop. It was close to 10:00 p.m., and I didn't like driving in the dark.

You and Seneca were riding with me. We thought you were going to sleep, so we were just going to run in quickly. But you started to get out of the car and got so angry at us.

It took both of us just to keep you sitting there. You had been sleeping on and off for the hour it took for us to get to the hospital.

I don't remember really ever thinking this would be the last time you sat next to me, so I could hold your hand while I was driving. But it was, and I never even knew it.

When we arrived at the hospital, I told you we were there. You got out of the truck and walked in.

They had a room ready for you, and you got up on the bed and laid down.

I remember the doctor asked how you got into the hospital if we had to get a wheelchair. No, Jeremy walked in on his own. We just supported him. He couldn't believe it because once you laid down, you became unresponsive to everyone in the room and your surroundings.

As soon as we arrived, a hospice personal came to talk with us. Your doctor told her at that time, you had never been interested in hospice, and the family was not interested in the services now. I was so impressed at how he was still honoring your wishes. We didn't want to talk to her anyways.

December 1, 2011

On December 1, I had talked with one of my coworkers again to keep them updated. They asked to share the note with the rest of the staff. It read, "I spoke with Val this morning, and Jeremy is in the hospital in Crookston. They were having a difficult time keeping him comfortable at home.

"They worked with home care last night to figure out a plan on what to do.

"Jeremy had been given less than a week, maybe only a couple days to live. They anticipated a day or so. The family would be staying at the hospital now until he passed."

Jeremy got anxious when there were a lot of people around, so if anyone wanted to go see them, please give Val a call first.

I hadn't even had the time to bring up how wonderful my coworkers had been over the last couple of weeks.

My friend Wendie had worked with many of them to arrange for food to be brought to us every couple of nights. So we had been blessed with some wonderful meals. Then she had a Christmas fund for the family so that we would still have a Christmas.

I had not been sure how we were going to do that since I would not be getting a check for some time. Actually I had no idea when I would get back to work and start getting a check again. So the money for Christmas would be a blessed gift.

Wendie had no idea how much of an angel she had become. The strange thing was she had it set up so that the coming week, we were scheduled to get meals every night. Funny how that worked out when we were going to be sitting up at the hospital.

Every night, someone from work stopped by. We had chili, hot dish, gift cards, and food all the time. The room you stayed in had another room attached, so we usually sat in there with the food and company. The nurses said it was always smelling so wonderful. Funny how the smells reminded us to eat.

The days in the hospital just seemed to have become a blur for me. You seemed to be resting much easier now. You woke up at times to eat and go to the bathroom. Sometimes you were able to visit with company.

Auntie Tammy had Bella for a couple of days. She had been so good to stay up here and help with you. One day, she even cleaned my house.

Your blood pressure remained low, not much change. Aunt Janie and Uncle Obie had stopped by, and the one day they were there, your eyes just popped open.

You looked at your aunt Janie, and the first thing you said was "Hello, beautiful." I thought it was so cute. However, when you were the one lying in the bed dying, you still tried to make other people feel special.

Wendie and Linda came every day to spend time with you. One night, when Linda was talking to the nurse, you asked her if she thought she was a nurse because of the questions she was asking. We all just laughed because she was just finishing up with her schooling.

Your feet and hands were turning purple when you sit up for too long. Your color was so much darker. It was so strange because your hair now looked like it was black.

This was one thing I noticed about you right away when I would walk into your room. Maybe it was the different lighting.

Your blood pressure had dropped today. It was now 80/38.

At times, you talked about things that didn't make any sense, but we usually just ignored that and tried to go along with whatever you say.

Your aunt Tammy was leaving today, so she came to say goodbye to you. How do you react when your sister comes to say her final goodbye to your son?

I cried as she hugged you and told you how she loved you. You told her you would see her again and then told us not to cry.

Mom was singing to you, and we thought you were sleeping. You leaned over and asked who was singing. I told you it was Grandma DeeDee, and you said, "Grandma has such a beautiful voice. She sounds like an angel." I wish Grandma would have heard you say it.

Your voice was so soft and tender when you were telling someone how much you love them.

Holly brought Lori up to see you today. Lori cried and wanted to just hug you.

We gave you time alone with each person that came. You hugged Lori and told her you loved her, then you told her not to cry. Sometimes when you would say don't cry, it just made the person cry more.

Seneca and I were trying hard to let everyone have their special time with you.

I know when you were with Lori, it would not have been the same for her if someone else had been sitting there. She was so young, and yet she remembered.

You woke up long enough to put your arms around her. You tried so hard to comfort her. I am going to miss you so much, my beautiful angel. You were everything a mother could ever want in a son.

I was thinking back to that day not long ago when you and I had gone to the lake alone. I had been hoping to have some time alone with you, so we could talk if you wanted to.

But in the last weeks, you really didn't talk about much. I remember asking you about being so angry and why you got so mad at me. You told me, "Mom, I love you, and I just wish things were different."

I remember the conversation about Bella, and all you said was "I know she will be taken care of." I wonder now what you thought would end up happening. I told you then I would make sure she was taken care of.

December 5, 2011

It was a quiet day in our little hospital rooms. It gave us time to clean up what we could and fold up blankets.

Seneca's parents had decided to return to St. Cloud. Denny left to go to work, and your dad and Karen were not there in the morning.

You slept most of the day today. Linda had stopped by and was able to get you to eat a little bit in the evening. Your brother Santos came up to visit with you. When

I told him you had been sleeping most of the day, he said he could wake you up.

So while my boss was there, Santos started his "your momma so ugly" jokes, trying to wake you up. He told you that your momma was ugly.

For some strange reason, you woke up to that and told him, "Your momma looks like a fag streetwalker." You did make us all laugh with that one.

Funny how Santos could bring out that sense of humor and your competition. You may not be brothers by blood, but love is thicker!

The two of you were always trying to get the best and last word in. You even insisted on getting up in the chair at one point today, just so your nurse could see you sitting up. You still fought very hard to make others think you were doing okay.

At one point when you had asked for something to drink, you were shaking, and Seneca and I both tried to help you hold your cup. You got angry with us and wanted to do it by yourself.

When I held the bottom of the glass, you asked if everyone had left. When I told you there was no one around, you then let me help you.

Pastor had stopped by, and during your conversation with him, you told him you loved him and how much his visits had meant to you. It touched his heart, and he came out of your room crying.

I wonder how many people you had really touched without even saying a word to them. I believe you are an angel to more people than just me.

December 6, 2011

You slept most of the day. You did get up to go to the bathroom once. The last time you got up was about 10:00 p.m.

Seneca and I happened to be in the room with you. You started to get mad at Seneca because you thought she had thrown some Styrofoam in the garbage. You told me to get her out of the room because she was making you so mad.

Seneca had done nothing to make you mad. You just woke up in a bad mood. You then had to stand up to go to the bathroom.

I stood by your side as you leaned up against me, and Seneca helped hold the urinal. I didn't know it then, but it was the last time you would get out of bed and the last time you would ever lean on your momma and put your arms around me. I should have held on to you longer.

Seneca, Denny, and I were the only ones here now.

December 7, 2011

On December 7, it was the day Jesus called your name, and you answered him.

Today you were unresponsive all day. Your doctor was in for a while this morning, and he tried to wake you up, but you didn't even respond to him. He said that tomorrow we had to move you downstairs to another room because of your insurance would not pay for a hospital bed any longer. The report was that your one lung was not working, and the other was filling up with fluid. Your kidneys had shut down.

I couldn't remember who stopped by today or what the day was like.

I remember sitting with you holding your hand. I measured your thumb and realized it was the same length as mine.

I looked at your beautiful eyelashes and wondered how they became so long. I tickled your cheek and thought back to the times I had done that to put you to sleep. I wondered if you would smile or ever udder the words I love you again. The day was a quiet one, and I know now that tomorrow may be full of more heartache more than I had ever known.

Late that evening, Wendie, Linda, and I had been sitting with you. You still had not responded to anyone. I realized that the blankets were bunched up under your back.

I remember thinking how uncomfortable that must be for you. So I asked the nurse to come in and adjust your blankets and see if she could maybe move you so you would be more comfortable. She told me they would be giving you a sponge bath at the same time. I was thinking maybe that would wake you up.

We walked around while the nurse was in the room with you. Wendie and I returned to your side. I noticed that your breathing had changed. You were taking short little breaths, and then you would stop for long periods of time.

This was it. Seneca and I decided it was time to make some phone calls to let family know we didn't think you would be with us very long.

Things from that time on just seemed to happen quickly. Maybe it was slow. I didn't really know. I just stayed close by and tried to pay attention to everything happening around me.

You started to moan and make some noises when you were breathing. Seneca and I started to wonder when the last time was that you had been given medication.

We knew it had been earlier in the day. I thought maybe the morphine would help you rest, maybe more peacefully. I didn't want you in any pain. Then your breathing changed again. I couldn't remember what it was like at that point, I just remember thinking you are resting so much easier now.

I looked around the room and Kevin and Karen, Wendie, Linda, your uncle Obie, Seneca, and I were in the room with you.

Seneca's parents were on their way here. Denny was at work and trying to get here. I know that Kayla and Matt were on their way, and so was Sheena.

I was leaning over the side of the bed holding your hand and rubbing your cheek with my other hand. All I could see was my baby lying there, and I thought you could sleep.

Honey, Mom is right here. I am not leaving you.

I remember whispering in your ear and telling you over and over again how much I love you.

I told you, Jerm, you can go home now. I will be joining you tomorrow. It's okay, baby. It's time to go home.

You started to move your body with every breath, and I remember at one point just leaving the room, I was so overwhelmed with emotions.

I just couldn't take it anymore. I didn't want to let you go, but now I had no choice.

Kayla arrived with Matt. She just crawled on the bed and laid next to you and hugged you. She told you she was there. It seemed like you took two more breaths, and you were gone. No more breathing, no more pain—nothing but peace.

Sheena arrived just minutes later. She was so hurt because she had not been there in time. Seneca's parents got to the hospital about half hour before you died.

You had people who loved you there until the end.

You were not alone. I promised I would never leave you, and I didn't. I stayed with you, baby, until the end, till your heart stopped beating, and mine was broken in two.

The pain of that moment was so intense. All I could do was push it away. I wanted to pretend like you were just sleeping.

Santos came shortly after everyone had left your room.

I was still in there with your dad Kevin.

Santos walked in the room. He looked at you and just said, "No, Mom, he can't be gone." But he knew. Never have I seen such tears and sadness in his eyes. He sat next to you and just cried.

Shortly after, your cousin Jesse arrived. He said he got there as soon as he could. I didn't ask how fast he had driven.

He wanted to be with you. He was so good.

You know, Jeremy, he stayed with you that night till four in the morning when the coroner finally was able to take you to Fosston. He said that the police have to stay with a body until the coroner arrives, and he wanted to be with you. He said it was hard, but he never complained. What a gift of love that was for him to do.

Denny came as soon as he could from work. But it was late when he arrived as well.

It was so difficult as each person trickled in to see you. It seemed like each time we stood by your bed and looked at your lifeless body, the knife twisted as my heartache grew.

Your head was laying off to the side, and your mouth was open slightly. I asked your dad if you could just move your head and get your mouth closed. He did, but he cried as he held your head in his hands.

Your hands turned color so quickly. I didn't want to stay there any longer. I wanted to just run out and not have to face any more of this pain.

I remember standing there looking at you lying there so still.

Your dad and I alone with you. When he hugged me, all I wanted to do was turn back time. I didn't feel grief; I felt alone. I wanted to go home.

You were an organ donor, so the hospital had to wait for someone to come up from Fargo and do the surgery to remove your corneas. They were donated so that someone would be able to see for Christmas. What a wonderful gift. Even in death, you were able to continue to give. Because of the cancer, they were unable to donate anything else.

December 8, 2011

December 8 started out kind of quiet. I couldn't really say I slept well last night.

We didn't get home till around one thirty in the morning. After everyone had stopped by the hospital, we sat in the visiting room for a short time—long enough for us all to clean up and move out.

We had been staying there for a week. Denny had his truck, and I had to drive home alone.

It was the longest drive I have ever taken. Part of me wanted to stay with you last night, and the other part of me couldn't handle watching the changes take place in your body.

I didn't like blue and the cold feeling. I knew it was just an empty body. Your soul is in heaven. You were not there anymore.

Grandma DeeDee and Grandpa Leif came over this morning. Linda and Wendie spent the day with me as well. I went over to Jen's and brought her your necklace.

Remember, it was the one she had bought you. You told her it had gotten lost. But you just forgot you had it hanging in the bedroom. She didn't know you still had it.

Jen left for the Mayo Clinic for her own health reasons on Tuesday. She was so thankful to have your necklace so she could bring it with.

I know it wasn't for good luck, but maybe I just felt like having a part of you there with her. Tomorrow we had to meet with the funeral home.

Seneca had been gone all day with Bella. When she came home, she said that your dad and Karen would be coming over to the house.

She then went downstairs with Bella. I didn't know it at the time, but I guess they had met earlier and planned on coming over to try to make plans. I felt like they were all there to lecture me. I was so surprised at the way they came in here.

Karen told Denny that he didn't have an opinion in anything that was said because he was the stepdad. Well, she was the stepmom, and she was already making rules.

Seneca and Kevin preceded to tell me that the funeral was going to be on Tuesday. We had always talked about having it on a Monday or a Friday so that family from a distance could attend and not feel so rushed.

But the funeral home had another funeral on Monday. Tuesday was the soonest they could do it. I just didn't want to have your funeral that quickly.

I know that after that day of the funeral, I would never see your face again, and you would be buried.

I really didn't want to say goodbye to you again. Kevin said that we couldn't wait until next Friday. I told them that I was not going to have anything to do with the plans. They had already talked and made up their mind.

Karen got upset with me at one point when I told them that I was the only one who had been here for you over the last twenty-five years.

I had never left you. Kevin had missed ten years of your life and now tried to act like he had always been concerned. Seneca had only been your wife for less than six months. Just weeks ago, she told Karen she only married you because of

Bella. I don't understand how a mother can just get pushed aside and no concerns as to my feelings.

I guess we would know more tomorrow after we had the meeting at the funeral home.

Seneca told me that the funeral home had called and asked for the clothes you would be wearing.

Auntie Tammy had given me a suit for you to be buried in. You didn't know it, but it had been hanging in the closet for the last six months.

I asked Seneca to get you a new shirt with a red tie. Since the church was already decorated for Christmas, maybe it would look nice for you to have some red.

Picking out clothes for someone to be buried in was not a pleasant job. I wanted to pick out one of your crazy T-shirts you always used to wear. The only problem was that I was afraid it would show up through your white shirt. The meeting at the funeral home went well. I have to admit that it felt like we were in a movie and just waiting for the rest of the show to play out. I couldn't say I was crying or feeling like it was real.

We talked about the casket and the flowers. They had a list of all the people we would need to send a thank-you to at the church.

Seneca would be taking care of that part. I said I would pay for the obituaries to be sent to the papers. We decided to all go together on the big flowers that draped over the casket.

I also asked the funeral home about having two baskets for cards at the funeral. I know it was not normal to do this, but I had had so many people talk to me already about making sure their card and gift go to us. My plan was if I have to fight for any legal stuff concerning Bella, that money will have to help to pay for it.

We did decide to have your funeral on Thursday, December 15. We couldn't wait till Friday just in case your body started to show signs of decay.

The planning seemed to fall into place. We wanted to have your funeral at the church you grew up in here in Fosston. But you had become so close with Pastor Strenge. We all wanted him to perform the ceremony.

Bethel church did agree to this plan. Kayla had been working so hard to get a video put together of your life.

We didn't know how many people to plan for, but it sounded like we could be having a very big funeral.

Seneca had to work on getting financial stuff taken care of. Her parents left today.

Bella's mother called again tonight—first time I had spoken with her in months. She basically wanted to know about you dying. I told her about the hospital stay and how difficult it had been. She seemed like she was concerned and said she was having a difficult time just thinking about you being gone.

At the end of the conversation, she asked about Bella. How do you tell someone how a two-and-a-half-year-old is dealing with the loss of her daddy?

Bella just knew that you are in heaven. I don't think there was anything else we could tell her right now.

I woke up on December 10 missing you so much. It had only been three days, and I missed the crazy life we had gotten used to.

I miss your sense of humor, your smile, and your laugh. My mind had so many memories, and I didn't ever want to forget.

I started to think about last Saturday when you were talking to your doctor about your medications. You were wondering if you were still getting all your meds because you hadn't been taking any pills.

Your famous quote that day was "Come on, Doc. I know you are giving me morphine, but I have not taken any pills, so how you are doing it?" I think of the look in your eyes and how serious you were at the time.

I miss those looks you would get when you wanted an answer right away. I guess you never thought about the IV as your medication line. Sometimes you were such a dork. Jen and Auntie Janie called today. They shared how they were missing you, and both were having a difficult time just thinking about you being gone.

Grandma DeeDee called and was talking about how they had come up to see you last Wednesday. She said she wanted to stay there. Grandpa Leif had thought they should leave. She felt so bad that she was not there for you at the end. I tried to let her know it was okay.

You had a room full of people who loved you, and you knew your grandparents were praying for you. There was nothing else your grandparents could have done.

Your grandparents came over that evening to visit. Grandpa Leif wanted Denny and I to play a game of Rook with them. It helped to do something normal to take our minds off the loss of you.

One of the neighbors came and stopped by the house to drop off a plate of cookies. What a thoughtful neighbor. Sheena, Kayla, Seneca, and I worked on your obituary tonight. I felt like there were no words to tell people what kind of a person you had become. Did other see the son I had?

Sunday morning came, and I could hear your voice asking, "If anyone wanted to go to church with you"— something you always asked on Sunday mornings.

I wish now I would have gone with you more often. I know after your dad and I were divorced, I hadn't gone to church much. But I always felt like I was being looked down on for going through a divorce, and I always felt alone with my five kids sitting there with me. I know this was just crap in my head, but it was real to me.

This never stopped the times we had to talk about our faith and what we believed in.

Denny and I did go to church in Clearbrook with Grandma DeeDee and Grandpa Leif today.

Great-grandma started to cry when she saw me walk in. She said her heart was breaking, and she knew you were with Grandpa Lester.

Many relatives stopped to share their condolences with us. It felt strange for people to tell me they were sorry. I just wanted you to come home. It was so quiet without you.

I wish you would have taken care of issues concerning the custody of Bella. I know you, Seneca, and I had talked about what could happen and what we should try to do, but you never wanted to get anything in writing. Guess part of that was because you didn't really want to believe that you would die.

Bella will grow up one day and wonder who she looked like and if she was wanted. She will have so many questions. I know because Santos and Lori did that after their mother died, and they lived with us. Bella will need contact with her family.

Seneca is young, and at some point, she will remarry and perhaps have children of her own.

I am not sure how Bella will fit into that life. I may not agree with her bio mothers parenting style, but I still think Bella needs to know her. I guess if she wants to fight for custody, I will have to get an attorney. At least if Bella is with us, she will be able to spend time with both of these people who love her.

I know this is what you wanted because that much we did talk about. At some point, Bella will have to decide where she wants to be and who's family she wishes to be part of. But I think if she is taken from one family or the other, she will grow to resent the separation.

I have to be the one to think with an open mind and not give in to any pressure. I know Seneca's family love Bella. She sees them as her grandparents and her uncles and her aunt.

She had a strong bond with Seneca. I don't want Bella to lose that. But it will have to be Seneca's responsibility to keep that bond strong.

One of the neighbors brought over a hot dish tonight.

It was so good.

Kayla and Seneca took Bella to see your grandma Myrtle and aunt Sue today. They must have stopped at your dad's as well and made more funeral plans.

They came home and told me who the pallbearers were going to be for your funeral—all your cousins on your dad's side, Jesse and Matt as well.

I really didn't have a say or opinion in the matter. I was not going to say anything. It just wasn't worth a fight.

You had had many people who have always been there for you. Not just in the last six months when you were sick but friends and family who were not afraid to see you and show their support during your fight with cancer.

I guess I just look at things differently—some of these things you could have talked about with Seneca or me. But like you said, you never talked about it because you said Seneca didn't want to hear it.

I sometimes wondered how many things went through your mind, and you never dared to say anything about. Like the day you started to talk about never seeing Bella grow up and have children of her own, you started the conversation, and Seneca told you it wasn't true. You knew then that you wouldn't see your daughter grow up, but she wouldn't let you talk about the fears, and thoughts you had. Not when I was around.

December 12, 2011

On December 12, I received a phone call from Bella's bio mom. Your ex-wife. She informed me that she plans to take Bella. I tried to talk to her, but she stated that Bella was young and would learn to adjust. She made it sound like she would be picking her up after the funeral. Of course she informed me that you had interfered with her bonding with Bella, and it was now her chance to get her daughter back.

It amazed me how some people never really looked at what their actions were. She never once made a comment to the fact that she had been moving from place to place every couple of months without leaving an address, at times moving in with her mother so she would have a place to stay or think that she had been able to contact you or me at any time to arrange to see her daughter but had never made the attempt.

I am sorry, but my thought is this: If you love your child, you will be there to spend time with them no matter where or for how long the time might be.

I had always been there with you through the years. I remember when you were with Bella's mom, and you moved in with me for a short time before you got your place. She already had two boys: one she would do anything for and another little boy she said she never bonded with. So he was left with her mother most of the time.

I know we didn't see him. How can you love one child and not the other, and how was Bella going to fit into that picture?

I was so scared that the day of your funeral, she would try to take Bella.

I called an attorney and asked to meet with him. I had to go pick out the flowers for your funeral today, but after that, I was going to talk to the attorney. Jen would be going with me.

The attorney talked like there would be no problem when it came to custody, although I was not looking forward to this battle at all.

I didn't like to hurt people or go to court. I was not looking forward to this at all. But I hated the fear of her coming to try to take Bella after your funeral. What kind of a person would do something like that? Really? I think Bella's mom was trying to make a life for herself with her boyfriend and her family.

She had made choices in the past, and they would be choices she would have to live with forever.

I didn't like the fact that they would have to come up in court.

The lawyer also told me that Seneca had no rights to Bella. She had never been a parent to a child of her own and had no blood relationship to Bella. He also talked about neither of them working and being able to support Bella in a stable home at this time.

I think this was going to make a lot of people mad because your dad's family really believed Bella should be with Seneca.

I was only doing what my heart was telling me to do.

They could get attorneys, and we could go to court.

Now I needed to come up with $3,000 for his fees. If this goes to trial, I will need another $3,000.

Right now, I just wanted the papers served before the funeral so that we did not have to worry about Bella. She had already been through enough tragedy in her short little life.

I found out today that Santos and Alisha were having another baby. She didn't know how far along she was. I guess she had a doctor appointment coming up the first part of January. That would be six grandbabies on our side of the family.

Uncle Kenny and Aunt Tammy called every day. They were both feeling so bad about not being here for your funeral.

Kenny had a doctor appointment that morning and would be leaving as soon as the appointment was done. He hoped to be here early enough to spend time with some of the family.

Uncle Mike and Aunt Janet came over in the evening as well. They wanted to talk about a headstone for your grave.

We talked about you being buried in Bagley next to your dad's parents. Everyone told me how much they missed you.

Seneca hadn't said anything to me. Neither had your dad.

I couldn't believe you really weren't going to come home. I felt like you had just gone to St. Cloud and would be home in a couple of days.

I know that wasn't real, but it was easier to believe that then to think I would never see you again.

Kayla went back home to Grand Forks; she would be back on the day of your funeral. I felt so alone when she left. I often sat in the living room and wondered if you were watching from up above.

During those times, I would go to your web page on Facebook and read all the notes that people had been writing. I knew I always thought I had a wonderful son, and you had such a big heart. But to read what your friends and others write about you was so wonderful. It made me feel so proud.

I copied a few of the posts just to share with others, hoping, one day, people will be able to use my son as others did.

I'll never forget, and hopefully one day, Bella will be able to read them as well. Maybe she will see the part of you that others loved.

To me, that week before your funeral, being able to go back and read the things people said and the love others had for you made me so proud of the man you had become. Your uncle Kenny had written a note for your funeral, but he wasn't able to make it there in time that day.

This is not goodbye, I'll be waiting.

This was the toughest battle I've had to face. We knew time was short, and I tried not to waste.

I cherished each moment I had with you. You lengthened my stay by your love and support.

Prayers you gave none were lost or sent in vain. Jesus heard them all, especially the ones that were sent on your knees. They blew right in throughout heaven's gates.

I wanted to thank all who helped me cope cleaning up my dirt and the messes I made, the visitors I had for telling me how much you loved me. I could feel your hurt.

This battle was tough. I gave it my all. I tried to hold on, but now I'm done.

God was so good to me, giving me twenty-five years. He gave me a lovely little girl as close to an angel as you can get, a wife who tried all she could, and parents and family who never quit believing.

I tried hard to hang on as long as I could, but Jesus was calling we all knew he would. I asked him to remind you how much I love you. He said they already know that's why they were there all the way through.

When the time came, I had no pain. There were no tears or sorrow here.

Please be ready for your day would come. I would wave you to *come this way.*

Please do not cry for me. I love you all. This life, as you know, is temporary, so until I see you again. I love you all. I think of Kenny sitting down and writing this for you.

I am sure he cried as he wrote it.

Kenny tried to come and visit as much as he could.

But working in South Dakota, he came when he could.

I would never forget the night you sat on the sofa with him, and you were trying to show him how flexible your nose was. You kept pushing your nose flat, and Kenny kept telling you to stop. You kept on just to tease him. We did get a video of that visit, and it still makes me laugh.

As the day of your funeral came closer, I seemed to be numb. I completed the daily tasks and helped with some of the plans.

I remember a conversation we had about where you would like to be buried. You and I had been sitting out on the deck that afternoon. You told me you didn't care if you were buried in an old grill. Because you said you wouldn't know anyway. So the casket doesn't need to be fancy or anything special.

We had two family plots that could be used for the burial. You chose the one in Bagley. So that was where you would be.

I talked with your dad about those arrangements as the burial plot had been given to him by his father.

Because you were having a county funeral, you would not have a fancy casket.

We were not allowed to have a viewing the night before the funeral because of the extra cost. So visitation would be before the funeral.

Now my caretaker side kicked in. This means we would be at the church for a few hours, and we would not have lunch until later in the afternoon. I decided I would just make up a bunch of sandwiches before going to the church. I could just keep them in the family room. At least, it would be enough to hold us over for a few hours.

We still had no idea how many people would attend the funeral, and I felt bad for the ladies of the church having to put on so much food for us.

I asked family members if they would be able to bring a salad to help out. I know this was not something people would normally do, but I worried about dumb things and just wanted to make sure everything went smoothly. At least, things on the outside would look normal to everyone there.

After the meeting with the attorney, I had been granted temporary custody of Bella. I know she would be home with us. This also meant that Seneca would not have her.

I feared the day of the funeral. What happens if I can't do this? I wanted to be strong for the rest of the family, but I didn't know how I would ever say goodbye to you. I didn't know what I would do when they close that lid forever. I felt like you would be home soon, and then I would wake up.

December 14, 2011

My anxiety was crazy. Your great aunts and uncles Obie, Janie, Laurie, and Hal, along with Grandma DeeDee and Grandpa Leif, came to the house with the pastor tonight. We talked about missing you and special memories.

Laurie talked about how she sat with you when Grandpa Lester was sick. We talked about how big your heart was, and if someone was feeling bad and sick, you wanted to be the first one to make them feel better. If that meant sitting at the hospital, talking on the phone, or just being there, you would do it.

You would get up in the morning when you were eighteen and sit with your great-grandpa at the hospital till it was time to work. Leave for work and sleep a couple hours, and you would start the day all over again. You did this for about a week when he died.

You had such patience and love. You never said a word. You were just there. I am sure he loved to have your company, and he was very happy to see you joining him in heaven.

Tomorrow would be the last time I ever saw your face. I remember that night as I went to bed, I fell asleep praying. I asked God to give me strength to make it through another day. I cried because I missed you, and I wanted you home.

That night was the last dream I had about you. You came and gave me comfort.

In the dream, I was leaning over the casket, crying and trying to tell you how much I loved you.

I looked around when I felt someone standing behind me. Your hand softly touched my shoulder. You asked me why I was crying. I didn't run to you; I didn't reach for you. I cried and told you, "Jeremy, you are dead."

Then you said, "No, Mom, I'm not. That isn't me lying there. It is only a shell."

I told you, "Jeremy, I held you and I heard your last breath."

You said, "Mom, I am not there. Go to the funeral and cry if you have to, but I am not there. I am home waiting for you."

I did not understand it while I was asleep, but when I woke up, it made more sense to me.

I tried to tell you how lonesome I was and how much I was hurting. You comforted me and promised it would be okay. You told me to be strong for the funeral but not to feel bad because it really wasn't you lying there.

The words you spoke in the dream: "I was home waiting for you." Those were the words I said when you died.

This dream it was so real. I could still see you telling me not to cry. I would be strong for you!

The day of your funeral, I had peace, and I was going to be fine. You were home. The morning was a rush, making up buns with egg salad and meat, getting everything done.

I was in such a hurry to get to the church that I had forgotten to make sure I looked okay.

Linda and Wendie had come to the house before going to the church. So they were parked behind my truck.

I had gone out to put the buns in the back of the truck, so I lifted the door and was pushing everything in the back. I could hear Wendie and Linda laughing, so I turned around to see what was so funny.

I had been in a hurry when I went to the bathroom, and my dress had gotten stuck inside my pantyhose. There was my butt exposed to the world. I was thinking you would have been laughing hard too. I just fixed it and shook my head at those two. They always seemed to have a way of making me see humor in the day.

I remember walking up to your casket and looking in.

This was the first time I had seen you in a week.

The dream from last night came to my mind. I know that was not you, but your body was lying there.

It helped to think that you were in heaven and not in the casket. I walked up to hold your hand; it was so cold. You looked so handsome in your suit, white shirt, and tie. You always liked to look good. You would have been proud of the way you looked today.

Your hair was so soft, and it laid on your forehead so perfectly. I think you were so handsome. I guess any mom would think that of her son.

I remember going to the casket one last time and kissing your head to say goodbye, your soft hair, and cold cheek.

The ceremony was so beautiful. Everyone had done such a wonderful job putting everything together.

Everyone enjoyed the video that Kayla had worked so hard to make. People said they cried when that song was played on the overhead "I Will Worship You."

Pastor Nate used to be your youth pastor when you were young.

During the time of your dad and I getting the divorce, he had been such a positive support for you. He flew here from Washington. I was so surprised to see him.

He had his dad with him, and he got up and talked about your relationship with God. How important that was to you.

Jeremy, the church was full. I couldn't believe all the people there. I didn't get the chance to talk to many, but to those I could talk to, I did.

Relatives came from the cities and far away, coworkers from both my work and your dad's.

It was amazing to see so much love and support. You would have loved all the attention today.

It was such a loving beautiful service, definitely a celebration of your life.

Your aunt Tammy had sent four roses up here, so I put them in the casket with you. One for each of her boys who were unable to be here today.

I remember feeling hurt and pushed aside when Seneca and her parents were to be ushered in before me. I thought, *How could this be? I am your mom.* She had only been your wife six months. But after I was told where to stand, I said no more and took my place in line.

After the service, we went to the cemetery.

It was the first cold day of the winter. When we returned to the church, so many people had already left. I didn't get to really talk to many of the family members who had come to the funeral. I had my little box of cards, and the day was over.

Seneca had the guest book. I never did see who that day had been there—the people I had missed.

When Seneca left, all I had were a few clothes left in your closet and the cards of sympathy. Everything you had collected for your daughter and you was gone. I would most likely never know what I or Bella would miss.

JEREMY TIM
BAUMANN
FOREVER IN OUR HEARTS
JUNE 10, 1986 – DEC. 7, 2011

CHAPTER 4

Making Changes

To think this was just the start of the rest of my life without you every day. I wish for you to be here.

I wish for one more hug, one more cup of coffee with you, one more "I love you, Mom." Maybe I wish for time to go back before we had to face this nightmare that has brought me here.

I wait for you to come through the door and tell me to "Wake up, Mom, I am here and always will be."

We had court this week for Bella. Her mom was served with her custody papers today. She sent me a note telling me how upset she was. She said she felt like I lied to her.

The attorney called and said I had custody of Bella till court on January 10.

I love Bella so much, but I do not like having to go to all this legal stuff.

I spent my day with Kenny and Kelly. We talked about the funeral and how many people had been here.

I couldn't remember if we watched the recording of your funeral online or not. It was nice that some of the church's record events like that now.

I know it was more emotional for me to watch that recording, then it was for me to sit there.

Thank you for coming to visit me in my sleep before your funeral. I think it helped me to survive the day so much easier.

I also went to visit with Mike and Janet over the weekend. It was nice to have family so supportive. I love that I am from a family like this who are always so close and just a phone call away.

Mike talked about you hunting and sitting in the little hunting shack waiting for your deer. He really wanted me to start looking at headstones for your grave. I was not ready for that yet. I was missing you so much.

Seneca said she was leaving with her sister tomorrow.

Not sure when she would be back.

I went to the cemetery to visit you. It was difficult to go there. I just couldn't really explain what it was like to go to a cemetery and to see your son's name on a freshly dug-up spot. I brought you three roses.

On that Sunday, Seneca had left for St. Cloud. Kenny and Kelly left for South Dakota. Denny returned to work. Bella asked about you today. I asked her who loves her.

She said, "My daddy."

I told her daddy would always love her.

We looked at pictures of you. She was excited when Denny came home from work. She loved him and enjoyed his attention.

Sheena came over and took Bella to her house for the evening to spend some time with her cousins.

December 25, 2011

December 25, 2011, was our first Christmas without you. I missed you ever day and so many of those days I spent crying.

I admit I need to find some strength and get past this empty feeling. But it was really hard to move forward. I couldn't imagine my life without you in it.

One day, Sheena came by, and we listened to your voice messages on her phone. Another day I read all your text messages you had sent me. I don't know if doing those things make it easier or not. But I don't want to forget your voice or the way you used to talk.

Jen came over on Thursday and gave me a Christmas card you had written on for me.

I cried for a long time. I think the thing that made me cry was not that you had written on the card. But the knowledge of how difficult it was for you to write something down and thinking you wouldn't be here to give it to me. It must have caused your heart to break. Just so you know, I will cherish that card for the rest of my life.

I ordered twenty coffee mugs with your picture on them to give to people as gifts this year. Now they would be able to have coffee with you in the morning.

I know I sure miss you in the mornings and many times when I am having my coffee. I looked over at the sofa and thought of you sitting there. Even at the end, you didn't always drink your coffee. Sometimes you just poured up a cup and would come sit with me.

I am going to admit, having a Christmas this year was the last thing I wanted to do. But I would look at the Christmas tree we put up. It was there because you wanted to be here for Christmas.

I know that it was not fair for me to put my grief first and the needs of the family second. So I had to suck it up and be the strong person you need me to be for your daughter.

Everyone was here for Christmas Eve this year.

You remember how the holidays were here? We spent the evening with the kids and grandkids—Christmas Day you would spend with your dad.

Denny made quilt racks for all the girls, and we sent one down for Seneca too. I had no idea he had been working on making them out in the garage.

Santos even came home this year. But it didn't feel the same without you here. I don't remember you ever missing Christmas with your mom. I missed you yelling at the kids and telling them to sit down so we could pass out the gifts. We still had no snow, and the weather had been around forty degrees outside. I think it was gloomy but maybe just because I feel alone.

I filled out paperwork with social services last week, so Bella didn't lose her insurance.

This was the first time I had to say the date you had died to someone. It felt so strange to say, "My son died on December 7."

I still must find day care for Bella. I think Seneca still planned to sell the trailer house. So much I want to tell you, but I am afraid to write it down.

December 26, 2011

On December 26, your cousin Heather picked up Bella to bring her down to see Seneca. It was hard to let her go. But I knew it was important for Seneca's family to spend time with her.

Bella needed to see Seneca as well. I never told you, but the day I told Seneca that I was keeping Bella was pretty traumatizing I think for Seneca.

I had not told her about going to the attorney and seeking custody of Bella. I think Seneca just thought she would take her to St. Cloud with her. But I knew I had to tell her before the funeral.

I told her that Bella's mom had called and planned to pick Bella up following the funeral.

I didn't want that to happen, so I had to get custody. I told her how the lawyer said she didn't have any rights to Bella even after being married to you.

I wanted to give Bella a balanced life, where she would be able to spend time with the people she wanted to surround herself with. That includes her mom, Seneca, or us. I really don't think Seneca ever agreed to this, but she knew I had custody and Bella would be with us.

I finally got day care lined up for Bella. I was so excited because the place was only three blocks from the house. I don't think they usually had many kids over there.

I think Bella would like being with other kids her age.

I had to get her into a routine and used to taking a nap.

She needed to have something she could count on being the same every day. It seemed as if life the last couple of months had been so unpredictable for her. I wonder how she would adjust to the new changes.

Work was expecting me to return. I told my boss that I really just need January off. I was just starting life with a two-year-old and needing to get her in a routine and day care arranged. I was told I needed another note from my doctor to get this approved.

I made it to the dentist. I was having a good day until they turned the gas on.

Once that started to work on me, I started to think of you, and yep, I was crying again. After that, I went to see my doctor to get a note for the month of January. To stay with Bella for a while until she got used to being home and attending day care.

I told Seneca that Bella would not be staying for long periods of time with her. Seneca got upset. My thought was if it wasn't for me fighting to keep Bella, Seneca wouldn't be seeing her at all.

I know Bella's mom would not allow those visits. I was trying to make sure Bella had both her mom and her step-mom in her life. I admired Seneca for taking the time to see Bella and keep her involved in her life.

Sometimes when I was going through these battles, I understood how difficult it was for you. I now understood why so many times you told me Seneca didn't understand and the comments you made about marriage.

You were right. Seneca did expect things to be her way. I was going to try very hard to teach Bella to respect people and appreciate even the little things in life. I didn't want for every visit to be a conflict; I would like everyone to just get along.

January 6, 2011

It was January 6, and we were starting a New Year. Bella and I were home alone to bring in New Year's

Eve. Denny had to work that night, and Lori was with Santos in Crookston.

I admit it had almost been a month, and I still missed you like crazy.

Bella and I looked at pictures, or I found some piece of paper you wrote a note on.

I still cried often. It wasn't getting any easier for me. I was so scared people would forget the son I had.

I wrote on your Facebook page about every week. Guess I should stop that because people would start thinking I was nuts. Just writing on your page makes me feel closer to you, like maybe you will read it.

I got all the thank-you notes written out. I cried again. I guess the part about writing those notes that was hard for me was I just realized how many people loved you and supported me.

Bella came home from St. Cloud with a cold. She had been up for three nights sleeping with me.

Last night was the first night I think she got a full night of sleep. Just so you know, she was adjusting well. But then I think there had been very few days of her life she hadn't seen me.

When you were a single dad, many times, she would be here with us. She didn't ask for you or Seneca.

She surprised me. At night, she usually just went and crawled into bed, and when she got up in the morning, she walked out into the living room or came and got me. I was the one adjusting to being a mom of a toddler again.

Just to give you a little update. The funeral actually got paid for by social services. Seneca was not responsible for that. I never knew if she sent out thank-you notes or if she sent checks to those who served at your funeral. I pray she did. She had not offered to help with any of the legal costs for Bella.

We had to pay all of those, and now the transmission needed to be replaced on my truck. I wish you were here now because you would know how to take care of this stuff. Seneca received money for the funeral along with your insurance. I know it was not much, but you always said it was going to Kayla. She was selling your trailer house now and would have that money.

Remember how you said that you still had the money from the benefit and wanted to help with the cost of the transmission for staying here? Well, that wasn't happening, and I did not get any help with the electric bill like you had agreed on.

Jeremy, not once has she put the needs of Bella first. Remember that night we were sitting in the basement talking about what would happen if we had to go to court? You said right in front of Seneca that we need to worry about Bella first to make sure that she would end up staying with family.

Seneca acted as if the conversation never happened. She demanded her time with Bella and didn't ask for any gas money when she did pick her up.

I know I didn't mean to talk so negative about her, but I just feel like I was getting stuck with so much expense and things that were promised I would never see. I miss you and wish you could just straighten things out.

Bella had claims on the guest bedroom now. I didn't have a dresser in there for her yet. She slept well and was back to taking naps again. The plan was to get her dresser soon and make that her own room.

I was rather scared to think of returning to work. I had been on half-time for so long, remembering when you and I talked about me returning to work full-time. You told me you wanted me to work part-time so I could take you to your doctor appointments.

You wanted me to be there for you. I did that and now to think of returning to work without even getting a phone call telling me you are sick or that you think you need to go to the doctor.

Once again, I realized how much your illness had even affected my work schedules. Now I had to try to figure out how to make that normal as well.

My life had been planned around you and being available for you. Now you don't need me. What am I supposed to do?

Kayla wrote on your Facebook page,

> I wish I could call you and tell you the
> news. Matt proposed last night. I know you
> would have some silly comment aside from
> bring happy for me. Don't worry, I'll save a spot
> for you in the wedding, I miss you every day.

Kayla had been busy planning her wedding and figuring out what she wanted.

I returned to work, and Bella adjusted to Grandma and Grandpa Bower as well as day care.

Lori continued with her behaviors, but she was also taking on the role of being a big sister to Bella.

The idea of a headstone at the grave site was still emotional for me, but I think it was time to start thinking about getting one.

I talked with Aunt Janet and Uncle Mike about it. Your uncle knew the man who made the headstones and felt he would be able to get me a good price.

Your uncle Mike seemed to know everyone and had connections everywhere. I don't know for sure how I would ever come up with something to write on the headstone—something that would forever be a reminder of you.

I found out that looking through pictures to find one to place on your headstone was so difficult. For the first time, I realized you were sick for a long time. I wonder why I never noticed it.

I finally decided on one that we had taken for your graduation. You looked healthy and happy back then.

This soon will become another cost I would have to take care of. I wondered why your dad and Seneca walked away, and when the financial burdens came up, I was left holding an empty wallet. How long would you go without a headstone if I didn't take care of it?

I sometimes cried just because I felt like I had so much that Denny and I had to care for. I really just wanted some support and someone to tell me they understood. But I didn't really think anyone understood.

Your uncle Mike pushed me to get the headstone done, and I was so glad he did.

Every time we sat down to work on it, I cried. But we picked out one to hold a picture of you and to have a flower vase attached.

CHAPTER 5

Our New Normal

I struggled with thoughts of how Bella was ever going to understand her family. She had a mother she seldom saw, but she was still her mom.

She had a stepmother who loves her like a mom and spends time with her every month.

She lived with a grandma and grandpa. She had her aunts and uncles and family spent time with—all people connected to you!

I finally decided to make her a little book with pictures of everyone and a time line of her life.

The love she was surrounded with would never end. My job was to make sure she always knew how much her daddy loved her. She loved the book and wanted to read it all the time when she was little.

Sometimes unexpectedly Bella came up with a memory of you, and it made me laugh.

One day, Denny was drinking from a cup. Bella said, "Remember my daddy used to drink from that cup, and one day, he got sick and puked in it."

On her first day of school as we were driving in the car, she asked me if you were watching her.

I told her, "If your daddy can watch you, he would be doing it every day."

Bella looked up to the sky and told me, "Grandma, Daddy can't see me today." I asked her why, and she told me, "The clouds are the floor of heaven. Today there are too many clouds, and Daddy won't be able to see through them."

I love things like this. She let me know she missed you, and I was keeping you alive in her memories.

Over time, I finally figured out that grief never goes away. Every person feels the pain, but we might not all feel it the same way.

I thank God that I have Bella. She looks at me with the same look in her eyes that you would get at times. Then I think a piece of your heart is here with her. A piece of my heart is there with you.

Time slips by, and tears still fall. Not as often, but the pain is still there. Normal will never be as it was. Sometimes change doesn't feel good, but it is a part of life.

Bella now called our place her home. She referred to us as Grandma and Papa. She was in head start in Fosston, and she loved every day with her teachers and new friends.

She got excited with every new thing she learned. At times, she would tell me, "I already know that."

She was so proud of writing her first and last name, learning to count and recognize the letters of the alphabet. She is a very smart little girl, and her thoughts are beyond her age.

Bella hadn't had much contact with her mom. I had brought Bella to see her on several occasions, but she had never made any attempts to see Bella.

We talked about her, and Bella told me she loved her mom.

Bella continued to see Seneca and spent time with her. She looked forward to those visits. I found myself not only caring for her as my daughter but giving her more and trying to make up for you not being here.

We ended up selling the house in town. I found after you died that even when changing a room or redecorating it, the memories didn't go away. I could still see you in pain on the sofa, sitting in your chair in the basement, or lying on the bed upstairs. Memories of you were everywhere.

Denny found a house on a lake, and we bought that. I walked through the lake house and think how much you would have loved it. I had pictures of you and Bella hanging up in the living room. I remember one day thinking I needed to update the pictures because Bella looked so little. Then I realized I would never be able to update your pictures.

Your dad has moved back to Maryland with Karen. I tried several times to get him to talk to me after you died, but it never happened.

I still longed for him to say the words. I knew how you felt, and I missed him too. I knew I would never hear it, so I finally stopped waiting.

Kayla and Matt had a beautiful wedding. She carried a necklace of yours in her bouquet, so you were right up front with her.

She looked so beautiful and happy. I know you must have seen her that day because I couldn't imagine you missing your sister's special day. Your little Bella was her flower girl, and she was beautiful. Bella loved to dress up. Damian walked with Bella up the aisle.

Sheena and Fred had been divorced. Sheena struggled with anxiety and depression now.

Some days were very difficult for her, but she took it a day at a time. The kids were getting so big.

At times, I think Damian looked like you. Genesis wanted to buy a Christmas present for you this year. With all the snow we had, I still hadn't brought it to the cemetery. I don't think Zoey remembers you, but she knows that Uncle Jeremy is Bella's daddy.

I didn't see much of your brother Santos, but every once in a while, he sent me a note online.

Lori was no longer home with Denny and me. Her behaviors of running away and stealing just became too difficult for me to deal with. She ended up in a foster home for a short time and right now was in a group home for girls. Not sure what the future holds or her. It is sad for me because all I ever wanted for Santos and Lori was to share our love and our family with them.

I never wanted for them to go into another foster home. I knew they would both want to be with their biological family when they grew up. I didn't think they would try to forget us. I still pray for them every day and always will.

I will have to admit that for me the biggest change had not been having a little girl. The anxiety I dealt with was the difficult part.

I didn't talk about it, but I knew people saw it.

I found myself staying home more often than I want to admit. This was not because I didn't want to be with people, but more because I didn't want to make anyone uncomfortable.

I still wanted to talk about you and remember you. I found that it was uncomfortable for people when I mention your name. Often they changed the subject or acted like you were not mentioned.

At times, I cried and felt the tears falling down my cheeks. I couldn't stop them from falling. I had been told I should be over this by now.

Grief has no time limit. Home is safe. I could cry and say your name. No one was uncomfortable here.

After seeing a movie one night, Bella had another one of her deep thoughts. She asked me, "If God was Jesus's daddy."

I told her he was.

Then she asked, "Who is Jesus's mommy?" I told her it was Mary.

So she said, "If God and Jesus are in heaven, where is Mary?"

I told her that Mary died and went to heaven too.

She thought about this for a while. Then she said, "I bet Jesus was happy to see his momma, and I bet Daddy will be happy to see you." I don't know how this child could come up with such deep thinking, but at times, she was able to amaze me.

You my son were in my heart before I knew you. You took a piece of me with you the day you died.

I will forever love you, and when the day comes that God calls me home, I will run to greet you. Your smile will be the first thing I long to see.

I wanted to share a few of the Facebook comments that had been left on your page over the last few years. I found comfort in looking back and seeing that your life had left an impact on so many people.

I miss you a little. I guess you could say a little too much, a little too often, and a little more each day!

I miss you, Jeremy, more every day. I thought it was supposed to be getting easier, but it's not.

There were so many things I wanted to call and tell you. I picked up my phone and realized I didn't have your new number. I love you, buddy.

I was going over the history from my Facebook, and I found a birthday wish you had left me. It read, "Happy president day tard!!! I think that's right…hmmmmm??? I'm not sure but happy whatever day it is LOL and Happy Birthday."

This was the thing that made me miss you the most—your personality.

It was a very boring world without you. I wish you were here to make more memories. I want you to see me graduate from college, get married, and have kids. You would have been a great uncle to them. I miss you ever day, and I can't wait to see your smiling face again.

Starting a new year without you sure doesn't seem right winter just seems extra cold and lonely.

I went to see you today, although I knew you weren't there. I felt a little closer to you for a moment.

I wish you were here to go on some crazy road trip with or sit and watch a movie with me like we do so many times, talking all night long about nothing at all. I wish I could have one more time to tell you what a special friend you were to me.

What I wouldn't give to hear you say, "Hey, beautiful" as I walk in the room.

Twice now I have looked down at my phone and seen that I called you. I don't know how since my phone was locked, but apparently, I really wanted to talk to you.

When God took you home, the world lost one amazing person. Prayers of healing to his family may the arms of God and his angels gave you comfort and love, strength, and healing during this very hard time.

I often sit and think of you, wondering if everyone knew how amazing you are. How many lives you touched here on Earth? Mine being one of them.

I know everyone has a special story or memory to tell, but when I think of mine, I still cried tears of joy that I met you. I felt compelled to write a thank you to Jeremy for all his prayers and stories he wanted me to tell my niece while she was recovering.

Jeremy had written a noted back to his friend, and part of it just touched my heart because it was his words of faith. I felt this was important to share because faith is so important.

I know you had sent me a thank you for
prayers and concern I shared with you. But it

is I who really want to thank you. I felt God had left my life for some time now. I had felt just empty and alone and thought God was far from me. When I heard your story God put it in my heart to go there and pray for her. I know now that God is still here in my life. He never left me, I left him. God is still here in my life. So thank you for bringing me back to God. Your friend Jeremy.

Jeremy's smile was one that lights up a room. He was the kind of friend that would do anything for someone without having to ask him for the help. He had such a kind heart.

I couldn't even bring myself to go to the funeral, Jeremy. I can't say goodbye to you. I can't imagine you not being here yet.

I took the day off to be there for your family like you were for my family when we needed it.

I wanted to tell them all about you and what a wonderful person your parents raised. But I couldn't make myself go.

I don't want to accept that your no longer here. I should be happy for you to finally be with the father in a place way better than here and that you aren't suffering any longer.

I knew you loved God, and I was thankful for the time I got to be with you. You made me a better person and taught me how to love people and how God works through us to touch others.

I'll see you again, Jeremy. I will take my time getting there. Know I will love you always my friend and thank you for everything you did here on Earth.

We have a hard time remembering how precious life is until it's taken from someone so young.

Spent so many years in school with you. I never took the time to get to know you, and now all I'm left with is those feelings of regret.

CHAPTER 6

Where Are You Now?

Over the years, I have found that God hasn't given up on us. I am so full of amazement when I have heard how you continue to touch lives.

God has been able to touch so many people through this book. I have never heard one negative comment.

Bella is now a teenager. She has been able to grow, and her daddy will always be her first love.

I want to share how God has been able to open our hearts and continues to show love through us after being with you through your cancer and watching you take your last breath.

I had a difficult time. I remember one time, Holly told me I should talk with another friend who had lost her son. At the time, I was not ready. I felt like her son had committed suicide, and this mom would have no idea what I was going through.

It took me a while to realize, it was not that her son wanted to die and mine wanted to live.

We were both moms who had lost our sons. Our grief was similar. I don't know what if things are easier for a person to die quickly, or if watching your child take their last breath is harder. Neither parent is able to make their child any better.

God has our days numbered before we are born. He knew while we were still being formed in our mothers.

I truly believe each child is a precious gift from God. Maybe a little baby who lived only a short time was really an angel who just wanted to feel a father or mother's love.

That child has a place in heaven and will be waiting for the day they can return that love. I know the grief is there, but sometimes we have to step back what did that life teach us.

I remember shortly after Jeremy died. My uncle was in the hospital dying. He was ninety-nine years old. He told me that God had forgotten to take him to heaven. My uncle must have felt some fear of dying. He told me the hospital was going to starve him to death.

I remember holding his hand and telling him I didn't believe that would happen. I told him he would fall asleep, and God would reach out his hand. I said, "Just reach back and grab it. You will be in heaven. "All the pain from earth will be gone." My uncle passed away the next day.

As the years went past, I believed I was getting stronger. I still struggle with going places and being around people. But I am able to go to work and enjoy touching the lives of people. I can't believe that I had been blessed with such a special job.

I don't know how, but I believe that God blessed me with a special gift: times that I just knew things.

I was never afraid of this, but if I tried to talk to anyone about it, they never understood. So it was easier to just keep some of it to myself.

The day your great-grandma Bergeson died was one of those days. I had a difficult time sleeping the night before. I am certain I had heard someone knocking on my door that night. But no one was there.

My grandma lived to be one hundred. My mom had called that day while I was at work, she told me Grandma wasn't doing well, and I should go up to the nursing home to see her.

I told my mom on the phone before I even left my office, "Grandma is going to die today. I know it."

I went up to sit with her, Aunt Janie, Obie, Grandma DeeDee, Grandpa Leif, Uncle Kenny, and Kelly—we all gathered in her room.

Grandma had gotten so skinny. I remember thinking I was leaning against the bed, but all I could feel was her hip bone.

She was taking her last breaths, and I sat holding her hand. Looking at the age and thinking of all her hands had gone through over one hundred years.

She was finally going to be of sound mind and body, and my grandpa was going to see his beautiful wife again.

The nurse came it to give her morphine. Grandma took her last breath, and she was gone.

I looked down, but to my shocking eyes, it was not my grandma lying there. My mind saw my son. I broke down. I couldn't breathe. The room was black, and I needed to run away, but there was no place to go.

I remember hiding in the bathroom, trying to breathe normally. I wanted everyone to just be busy. I had to leave. I wanted to go home.

Home is safe. This was the first time I realized I had hidden deep inside of me—all the pain and grief I felt the day you died. It was such a difficult day.

I know that Bella has attended several funerals since the day we lost you. I think for a short time, she really couldn't figure out what was going on. One day, we went to a funeral, and she was so curious about the person in the casket.

I remember telling her she could go up and look at him. I told her his heart was in heaven. it was just his body there. She was so excited that night when she came home. I think she told everyone that her daddy's heart was in heaven.

I don't know if I said the right or the wrong thing. I have a habit of just saying whatever comes to my mind at times.

I remember when you were little, Kayla was three that year. Your grandpa Floyd had died.

We told you kids that we had gone to the funeral home to pick out a bed for Grandpa to sleep in. You kids had a dog who had been hit by a car about the same time. When I told you guys that the dog was in heaven, you never saw him again. I wonder if Kayla was trying to figure out what had happened to her grandpa at that time.

I just remember when we walked into the funeral home, Kayla saw the casket and started to cry. She yelled at me, telling me I lied. She told me, "Grandpa couldn't be in heaven because he was lying in the bed." We had picked out for him. I don't think I handled it very well with her.

We enjoyed living on the lake. Denny always wanted to be the first one on the lake in the spring. As soon as the ice started to melt along the lake, he would get in his canoe and paddle around.

He was always so proud of being out there first. Sad thing was no one else knew or noticed that he was first.

Bella had a room in the loft, and she was always able to hear us in the living room.

Bella told me one day that she will always call me Grandma because a grandma is so much better than a mom.

She continued to come up with crazy little ideas as she has been growing.

One day, it was snowing, and she didn't want to come in the house. I asked her what she was doing, and she told me she was making a heart in the snow as big as she could so that you could see it in heaven.

I saved a little note she had written about having wings and flying to heaven to see her daddy.

My parents were getting older, and my dad decided to sell the house they had bought and remodeled. I don't know where the thought came from or if it was just a crazy idea I came up with.

But we talked with my parents and ended up getting a camper for them to live in. We had it close to the house so we could get the cable out there and they could have TV.

We had the electrician come and hook up an electric box for them. The first months went really good. Denny built a deck on the front of the camper, and we put up a shelter so their car would be protected.

We tried so hard to make my parents comfortable.

This worked until it became cold.

My parents ended up in the house with us. Now we have my parents along with Bella. Not always a good match, it seemed we did not parent the same way; and many times, Bella was stuck in the middle.

My dad was having a difficult time with the steps, and we knew we would have to come up with a better plan.

Mom didn't want to move to a small apartment, they had tried that before. Dad was easy going and was willing to do whatever he could to make my mom comfortable. They had developed a little routine.

They would go to church on Sundays, and Bella would often go with them. They would drive over and visit with my brothers often.

I think my dad made daily trips just to see how his boys were doing. When he would come home, they always enjoyed going out to eat. Some nights, we would play a game of Rook as our entertainment.

Denny and I decided that we needed to make some changes if my parents were going to live with us. We decided to move. We needed a house where my dad didn't have any steps to go up. His knees get stiff and cause him pain.

We found another house to buy, it was in the country, and I know my mom was not happy with that.

We had a bedroom built on the first floor and added a bathroom so they could have their own space. Denny put a deck on the front of the house with a ramp so my dad didn't have to worry about the steps.

My dad would watch Denny mowing the large yard in the summer. He wanted to help out around the yard, so driving the lawn mower became a job my dad loved to do. The first year was fairly easy for him. Denny just made sure that he went around the rocks in the yard before my dad went out. I could still see him on the mower, looking up at me when I would come home from work, and he would wave.

The second year my dad asked me if he had ever been on the riding lawn mower at the house before. It was hard to see his memory starting to fade. He had come up with one name that he used for mom, myself, and Bella. When he wanted one of us or something, he would just yell out "Dolly." Over time, we all were trained to answer to that name. But my mom was always Dolly number one.

One day, I had come home from work, and my dad was out on the lawn mower. He was stuck on a little drainage area. He was waving for me to come and help him. I ran to him and tried to push. But I couldn't move it. Finally, I had to tell my dad it would be much easier to push if you weren't sitting on the mower. He just giggled and got off. I was able to get it pushed out. Memories like that are just too good to let go.

I am not going to say that everything was perfect in our home. I don't believe in anything being perfect. Because about the time you say the words, disaster strikes like the time the tornado hit our lake property. You go sailing along, and things are great until the big wind comes and brings you back to reality. Sometimes I think it is just a reminder to us that we are not always in control. God is greater!

COVID came into our lives as it did around the world. Politics are becoming a subject people don't dare to talk about.

It seems like the world is changing. Again, you realize that things will never be the same.

I don't like it, and some of the changes seem to be just made-up.

Racism isn't a thing until you make it one. Just to be clear, everything goes two ways. Parents need to teach their children; we all bleed the same blood.

Bella had gone through a difficult year, and riding the bus alone became a nightmare for her.

I had to start working from home. My parents loved it even if I was upstairs in my little hidden office area, they always knew they could just yell up the stairs to me.

My dad would often say, "You have been up there long enough now. It's time to come downstairs."

I don't know if he or my mom ever see me as an adult or if I am still ten in their eyes.

One Sunday, my dad got up early and was getting ready to go to church. He had taken a shower and was a dressed to go. Mom got ready and was wearing an outfit that matched my dad's. They always had to match on Sunday's when they went to church, just a cute thing they did.

After church when they were getting ready to leave, my dad lost his balance. He couldn't really tell us what had happened. But by the time they got home, he said he was in pain. He complained of his arm hurting.

He was sitting in his chair and looked over at me. There was nothing I could do. I knew that look. He said he wanted me to call the ambulance. He didn't think he could get in the car. My heart was breaking, and I had to hide it. He became weaker even while he was in the hospital.

They told us he had gotten some virus which attacked his muscles. When the hospital released my dad, he was happy to be home. But life once again was going to take a major change for our family.

I had to stop and once again look at what was more important for me.

I had been at my job for twenty years. I had tried to work over the months that Jeremy had been sick, and I stayed home with him such a short time.

Our family is our life. Denny and I talked again about my need for going to work. I always feel like God was going to work things out. So if I retire to stay home and help with my dad, I have to trust that God will take care of us. I made the call, and in August, I would retire.

Around the same time, my daughter Sheena was trying to take care of a cousins four children, who had been placed up for adoption. Sheena had three girls and was not able to keep the little boy. Denny and I talked about it, and he was a year ahead of Bella in school. So we got our foster/adoptive license and decided to take him in. At times, Addison had given us a few challenges to deal with, but he was still here. We were waiting for the adoption to go through with him.

Our dog Shaggy is getting old. He is now blind and hard of hearing. At times, he just sits and stares at the wall. My dad and Shaggy started to have such a strong bond over the last couple of months. When my dad was in the hospital, we would try to set up visits for my dad to see Shaggy.

At times, we would just bring Shaggy to my dad's window so he could look outside to see the dog.

I really believe that animals are important for people who are sick or dying. When my dad came home from the hospital and would sit in his chair, he would have Shaggy sit with him, and my dad would just move his little finger to pet the dog.

The virus had done damage to my dad he had become so weak. We ended up having a physical therapist and a nurse come to the house weekly to work with him.

Denny and I would work together to lift him from a chair and get him to the bathroom. My mom often would feed him because he couldn't lift his arm.

One night, he had been tired, and we had gotten dad into his bed. He was just lying on his back with his eyes open looking up to the ceiling.

I laid next to my dad and asked him what he was thinking about. He told me how being a dad he always wanted to be the one to take care of his family, he cried and told me it is so hard for him when we have to be the ones taking care of him. I just hugged him and told him, "It was all in love." I told my dad I loved him and went to bed.

My dad was my hero, if I couldn't be like him, I wanted a husband to be like him.

One morning, I got up and went to the bedroom to check on my dad. I didn't see him in the bed. I asked my mom where he was, and she said she had checked on him about half hour before and he had been sleeping. I returned to the bedroom, and I found my dad lying on the floor up against a wall.

I had no idea how he even got over that far to actually fall off the bed. He had hit his head on a small table, and he was bleeding. But lying under the bed, licking my dad's hand was my dog Shaggy. My dad said Shaggy had been with him the entire time.

I have to share this one memory.

My sister Tammy and her husband had come up to stay over a weekend, and at times Tammy would just stay here and help with Dad. My dad couldn't walk, and he didn't have the strength to use his walker. Denny decided to walk on one side. I was going to support the other side. My sister decided to crawl on the floor under my dad to get him to bend his knees.

We all had a job to do. As we got closer to the bedroom, I think Denny asked my dad how he was doing, and my dad said he was doing pretty good. I told Denny I was doing fine and could make it the rest of the way.

Tammy looked up from under my dad and told us she was fine. We just about died laughing because my dad was no longer walking. He was riding on my sisters back.

We did learn that caregiving can give you such wonderful memories, and what a way to show your parent that you love them.

Kenny had gone with dad to his doctor appointment. During the appointment, Dad asked the doctor if he was going to make it to his ninetieth birthday. He told my dad he didn't think he had to worry about it because my dad was doing good. Even the therapist had been to the house and told him he had completed his goals. He was still having some pain in his muscles, but he was walking and feeling much better.

I had been done with work for about six weeks at that point. My parents enjoyed going for drives and going to visit. They had decided that afternoon to go to my brother Mike's house. He only lives about seven miles from us. When my parents were on the way home, my dad had a massive heart attack. He didn't make it home. They ended up taking him by ambulance to Bemidji hospital.

The ER spent fifteen minutes trying to get his heart to beat again. I really don't remember all that happened that day. It was not a good day.

My sister Tammy had been at the hospital with my mom. I remember everyone being called to come and meet with the doctors.

I think we needed to be there around three.

My dad was alive because of the machines breathing for him. We all knew he would not want to be laying there like that. Doctors said he had died from the heart attack, and they didn't know if he had any damage from that.

The choice was made to shut the machines down. I may not have all the information correct, but I was trying to put the pieces together the best I could.

Dad was lying in his bed, and the machines had been shut off. I decided to go home and would come back if I was needed later.

I know that, at one time, my mom and Kelly had been sitting with my dad, and my mom said dad lifted his hand and waved at her. He was never alone. I had been called and took off to get to Bemidji. I only had a half-hour drive, but it was dark, and the deer were out.

I wasn't even three miles from my house, when a big eight-point buck jumped on top of my little white mustang. My hood was trashed, and my car was going no place.

I had to call and ask my husband to bring me to Bemidji. When we got there, Mom and Tammy were in the sitting room. My nephew Jesse was sitting with my dad. I walked over to my dad to tickle his little bald head. He liked to be tickled. I knew my dad didn't have long left, he was having a difficult time breathing, and his mouth was open. His body was moving with every breath he took.

Jesse and I talked about the music my dad liked to listen to, and Jesse pulled up one of dad's favorite songs. We put the phone next to dad's ear so he could listen to the music. Soon he began to go without taking a breath. Jesse and I knew his time was short.

We played the song again for him. I tickled my dad and told him that I loved him. The song ended, and he never took another breath. We asked the nurse to go and let my mom know. She and Tammy came into the room and said their goodbyes.

I didn't mention that Tammy had lost her youngest son Logan just a year before. He had died in a car accident.

So to think that my dad had two grandchildren waiting for him in heaven, gave me peace. I know those boys would be so happy to see their grandpa.

About a year later, we lost my youngest brother Tony. The loss leaves your heart broken and your mind wondering how you will ever make it without these people there to make memories and share your love. But we make it because we have others that still need us.

I remember telling Jeremy that God doesn't take us until our job on Earth is done. Find your job and do it the best to your ability.

I received a phone call one day out of the blue. As another little boy I had worked with, said he didn't have any place to go, and he wanted to know if he could come and live with us as well. I told Dakota I would do whatever I could to make his dream come true. It took about a year, and we were able to get custody of him as well.

I know being a caregiver is what I do. I would never have picked that role for me, but God had different plans.

The pain and hurt never really goes away. It seems to me it just gets put on the back of our minds.

When memories come back, the pain is there. But I know in heaven there are no more tears. the wounds are all healed.

ABOUT THE AUTHOR

Val Bower wants you all to know she is no different than you are. She was blessed to be raised in a Christian home. She was the middle child, having two older brothers, a younger sister, and a little brother. She has been so lucky that they have all been close to each other. She has been able to learn that having family and friends in your time of need is a wonderful gift.

She has three biological children, two adopted children, three children she has custody of who she has raised as her own. She has four stepchildren. She has spent the majority of her adult life taking care of people who have needed her. Usually, a little bit of stress has been a good motivator for her.

When Val heard the word *cancer* and the doctor talking about her son, her mind did not want to accept the news. When she heard them tell her, her son only had a few weeks to live, she wanted to run away and not be found. But she knew he needed her, and she would not leave his side.

Her deepest wish is that after reading this book, moms and dads that you will hold your babies more often. Sisters and brothers will say "I love you" and mean it.

She wishes for families to realize that tomorrow may not come. Every day should have a memory to hang on to. Not all cancer is fatal, but it is always serious. Her mother, nephew, son, and daughter have all had to deal with cancer in some form.

God will heal you here on Earth, or you will be healed in heaven. Either way, she believes God is in control.